GRANDMOTHER DIVIDED BY MONKEY
EQUALS OUTER SPACE

Nora Chassler was born in Madison, Wisconsin, in 1972, and grew up in New York City. She has an undergraduate degree in English from Hunter College, CUNY, in New York, and a Masters in Creative Writing from St Andrews. She has worked as a model and a social worker. She lives in Edinburgh. Her first novel, *Miss Thing*, was published by Two Ravens Press in 2010.

by the same author

MISS THING

Grandmother Divided by Monkey Equals Outer Space

Nora Chassler

Valley Press

First published in 2015 by Valley Press
Woodend, The Crescent, Scarborough, YO11 2PW
www.valleypressuk.com

First edition, first printing (February 2015)

ISBN 978-1-908853-45-5
Cat. no. VP0065

A CIP record for this book is available from the British Library.

Printed and bound in the EU by Pulsio, Paris.

Cover illustration by Megan Burt
Based on a photograph by Steven Siegel

www.valleypressuk.com/authors/norachassler

Contents

for Frances and Don

Prologue

VIVIAN, THREE-INCH make-up wand poised, opened her eyes wide in the Maybelline compact to put on her blue mascara. Then – feeling the sunset on her smooth thick skin – she returned the little brush to its place on the floor without having used it. It was the eighth item in the clock-circle of pots, wands and compacts that were arranged around her. Viv was sitting Indian-style in the center of the circle, still holding her small pisshole-in-the-snow-eyes (as her dead father had called them) as wide as they would go. Then she rose very slowly, her too-small head held very straight – as if she were balancing a book on it, like a girl practicing for the Miss America title – and walked over to her big curved bay window.

Her face is tighter than when we'll see it next, but less sharp. She's coated in a layer of dishwashing liquid and 50s kitchen radio. But the soft cheeks don't hide the look she'll still have 16 years later – the look that makes her appear always to be plotting something. Viv stood straight and motionless at the open window that faced the Hudson River and New Jersey, which had only Palisades, and no highrises yet. She listened to the rhythm of the needle hitting the end of side 1 of *The Freewheelin' Bob Dylan*, over and over and over again.

Viv waited. She drank some Tropicana out of the carton (the one with the racist graphic of the native girl in a grass skirt, with huge eyes and a basket of oranges balanced on her head). She followed the progress of a rusty, high-heaped garbage barge ploughing downtown in the wine-red river,

9

the seagulls circling above it, as if on stiff wires. *Thank God,* she thought, as the last thick drip of orange juice slid to the back of her throat. It'd been six years, and there were several moments every day where she actually *thanked god* to be out of her mother's house. Viv ripped a piece of paper from a composition book that was on the sill, got to her knees above the *rat-he-ate-her* so she could see the river, and wrote:

September 30

103rd Street

Mudda Dear,

In answer to your repeated queries, I am doing very well.

I have a new job that lacks the cachet of social worker, but it is lucrative and less emotionally taxing. I'm glad I switched. I'm a bartender now at The Gold Rail, which is a few steps from Columbia. I meet 'many interesting people' and get to listen in on, if not take part in, their conversations. Yesterday I served <u>Allen Ginsberg</u> a beer. You probably don't know who he is. A very famous beatnik poet.

Oh, please stop worrying about me! I worry about you worrying about me, and that makes it into an infinity mirror. Remember the one I made in shop class in high school? I have three big boy roommates to protect me. Maynard Candy, Dick Grouse, and Johnny Madrid. They all want to meet you. I showed them your photograph and told them what a great dancer you are. I wish you could see my view. It is sunset right now. I wish it could be right now forever. The sky is red red red. There is a barge on the river. If I lean, I can see the tops of the heads of a large Hasidic family walking down below in Riverside Park. The sunlight is filtering down on their heads through the sycamore leaves.

And I do 'have plans'. I plan to marry. The smartest fella I can find, preferably a Jew. Then I'll live a life of unconventional me-

diocrity, here, where I may go unnoticed... But seriously, I <u>have</u> plans, but I think if I tell you it will jinx 'em...

Please find enclosed the 75 dollars I owe you.

Give my unkind regards to your wretched husband Norman.

Love your dotta,
Vivvy

PS: And now I think to add: I LOVE NEW YORK. I AM IN LOVE WITH NEW YORK MOM!

Kooky, Viv's first cat, came and rubbed her body back and forth along Viv's Levis, then jumped up onto the windowsill and disappeared from sight. Outside, the cat took the corner of the loose limestone gingerly – the masonry shifted a tiny bit – and she smelled the high air: a barbecue; pigeon's under-feathers; cigarette smoke; exhaust; then she climbed through the neighbor's window, where she liked to sleep on a patterned, threadbare velvet cushion.

Viv lit the half-a-joint she'd been saving. The cherry was like the bottom of a tiny rocket blasting off. She stopped looking out the window. She paced around in figure eights on the polished wood floor, sang a tune to the perpetually ending record *(Oh Maybelline, why can't you be true!)* and took a little book from the shelf, black and white and the size of a sandwich. She'd been in a barbershop quartet in high school, and she now read a poem aloud in a strong, confident voice, her chest pressed forward slightly. She attempted Allen's accent: 'Who kailled the poorwk chaaps? What price banaaanas? Are you my ain-gel?'

One of her roommates – the well-known transvestite Johnny Madrid – came in quietly, in a coffee stained silk shirt that he'd been wearing for three days, beard growth on his shiny chin, and surprised her. They kissed – one pretty and one pockmarked cheek – and said 'Hello DAHling.' Johnny grabbed the book, and did a perfect Ginsberg imitation. He had had the pleasure.

Then they ate some liver and bacon and onions that Viv fried, and each drank a glass of V8 juice. When Kooky smelled the liver, she came back in and had some too. After eating, Viv picked up her circle of dimestore chemicals, because Johnny had to practice his Rosemary Clooney sketch in the living room. Viv (slightly deflated; *why? why?* she didn't know) went into her tiny bedroom that faced the air-shaft, took off her jeans and sailor shirt and pulled a very short, red, stiff velvet dress over her head.

On her way to meet her friend Carol – with whom she was going to see a new folk act at the Tin Pan Alley – Viv decided to stop at the Woolworth's on 110th and Broadway. It was often this way: Viv was ready too early. For several years now, she'd been pacing – at the moment around her tiny corridor of a room, to give Johnny and the others some space. Before that she paced her dorm room at Vassar. Before that, her mother's bathroom. She was always waiting for something to happen, even once she *got* where she was going – to the party or gig or play or BBQ. The fact that nothing ever *did* happen was something she'd spend many more hours wondering about later. She'd cataloged thousands of 'mistakes'. The blame was always to be found in some detail. She'd chosen the wrong dress, or thought the wrong thought at the wrong moment, or eaten liver and onions. Walking uptown in the dusk, she saw the street lamps switch on, and realized she had a 100% chance of ending up disappointed again, tonight. The fact that it had taken her ten years to notice the pattern struck her as hilarious. She was thinking all this as she pushed open the clammy glass door into Woolworth's.

They were mopping up and turning off the lights. Closing time. Viv and an old lady stood over the clearance bin, eyeing the dying plants, discontinued lipstick shades and expired fishfood. The old lady, whose hair was dyed a bizarre aquamarine and who wore pointy cat's-eye glasses with green lenses, picked up a clear crystal ball the size of a canteloupe. It was an ornament for an 'executive' fish tank. She dragged her glasses to the tip of her nose, and studied and hefted the ball. She looked up and Viv was staring at her. They eyed each other. Neither was the type to back down.

'Fish enthusiast?' asked Viv.

'I'm a psychic.'

'Boloney.' Viv snorted.

The weird old lady put her open hand over her eyes, palm out, and ran it past her face in an 'Orientalist' fashion, the way a belly dancer does in a James Bond Movie.

'Ok, tell me my future.'

The 'psychic' squinted into the ball.

Then someone noticed them. 'Woolworth closing now, *señoras*,' the voice said, and hit the lights.

They stayed put over the dark octagonal bargain bin, shiny artifacts within caught the remaining light.

The old lady zoomed her head closer and further from the fish-tank thingee, as if demolishing an invisible obstacle. 'I see ... I see ... I see *a lotta* bullshit.'

'Ha!'

'Ha ha ha ha!'

'Alright girls, closing now!'

After she left Woolworth's, empty-handed, Viv wandered around in Riverside Park, not wanting to show up at Carol's too early. All the fucking waiting! The bullshit! That was the truth. In the dark and empty park, she set about pacing and smoked a Lucky Strike. She thought about a short story she might write. She'd call it: 'The Night of the Lost Iguana'. It would be about the time Dick Grouse's iguana escaped, about the slow, fruitless search that ensued. It would be a sad story, told from the dead iguana's point of view. She was still stoned as she paced in circles under the lamp, keeping just outside the light on the ground. She wished she had more pot. She thought, why can't you just be stoned *all the time*? Where is it fucking written?

1. Chapter Zero

How I have loved you Arnold Woods

… was written on the front of a paper plate that had been folded in half to make a card. It was written in a child's neat-but-shaky script, traced first in No.2 pencil, and then outlined in police-blue magic marker. Inside the card was a picture in green, ochre and red colored pencil. The paraffin – or whatever they make colored pencils out of – would not adhere well to the greaseproof surface of the picnic plate. In her attempt to make the colours stick, the artist had punctured the surface.

Arnie Woods, the man himself, turned the crimp-edged plate clockwise forty-five degrees, and exhaled a Puff-the-Magic-Dragon's nostril-load of Merit Ultra Light cigarette smoke. He spread his fingers wide to the edges of the plate, and was struck by the shape of his hand that way: that was how he used to hold a basketball with just his fingertips at Princeton High. And also – the way it looked hooked over the back of someone's hip. He'd graduated two years ago. Shit, time flies! He couldn't figure out what the fucking drawing was of. He twisted the plate the full hundred and eighty degrees.

It was a horseshoe shape … There were three very faint … daisies! stuck in the green hill, which was just one humped line, with a … tombstone! on it, like a crooked hat on a snowman. On it he could barely make out the words: *Epitath Carrie Martian. Born October 9, 1971. Died – TBA.*

Kids these days. So morose.

On the last day of school, Arnie streaked through the

cafeteria of Princeton High with four friends. They threw themselves buck naked, head first, into a caramel-colored van; it had a bulging, heart-shaped, tinted little window. It was revving at the exit by the baseball diamond. The plates had been doctored by Fat Lilith – the getaway driver and Arnie's helpful girlfriend – to read HA HA HA. New Jersey, ha-fucking ha-ha.

Arnie took another Merit out of the dirty breast pocket of his white button-down 50/50 Van Heusen work shirt and lit it with the stub he was smoking, while watching himself in the four-foot mirror that was propped above a little desk, bearing: a Panasonic answering machine the size of a shoebox; a Cinzano ashtray with ten marijuana roaches; an empty Tropicana carton, its lips ripped into a grimace; a tiny, novelty deck of Alice in Wonderland playing cards; a hairclip made out of iridescent pink fake shells; a pair of rusty tweezers; a two-year-old report card belonging to the artist Carrie Martian's brother Eli Martian; a half-scrolled newspaper clipping with FUNNY! written in the margin; a homemade cassette tape of Gilbert and Sullivan's *Mikado* 'Live at Symphony Space', and … lots of other shit. Arnie turned away from the mirror, though he would have liked to continue to admire himself. The mirror was next to the big windows that faced the courtyard and its weirdly light-reflecting, dun-colored bricks; the morning sun poured over the roof one floor up, on twelve. He had a cocaine hangover. And it hurt.

Arnold's girlfriend Vivian, Carrie's mother, worked part time at Macy's in Herald Square at the Self Center, which was a health food shop within the department store. She'd be home after picking the kids up, 4-ish, but Arnie would be back at work by then. He was hungry and nauseous. He noticed a gap in the guy across the courtyard's Levelors. Yes, he was *certain* Phil Silver – the neighbor across the courtyard, a cameraman for Sesame Street – was pointing a Super8 at him through a hitherto non-existent crack. Arnie unfurled Viv's bamboo blinds.

God, was his hangover creeping up. Total fucking para-
noia. The room was so bright, even with the blinds drawn.
So he tried to relax, to think of what he wanted to do, something he couldn't usually do except when he was alone in
the two rooms. It occurred to him he might try masturbating
– it'd been ages.

He closed his eyes. The hot pink of his lids burned. He
kept them scrunched, and groped around the cluttered
surfaces for his tortoiseshell Ray-Ban Wayfarers. When he
found them on the mantle over the nonworking fireplace,
he stuck them on, opened his eyes, and fell back on the itchy
mustard fold-out sofa-bed he had helped Viv salvage from
the garbage on 71st Street last week. Just last week. Last
week it was summer; and now … it was still hot, it still felt
like summer, but Carrie and Eli were back in school, and
they were talking about the Halloween parade and who
they would be.

Viv had a great body for a forty year-old, undeniably. Her
arms with the dowel-like, graspable wrists; the warm skin
behind her tan elbows, thin and soft like under-feathers.
Arnie stared at the smoke rising and pooling at the level of
the molding, just beneath the ceiling, and put his hand under
his shirt onto his warm, concave stomach. He recalled Viv's
bicep, almost masculine, it was so well-defined; her under-
arm, where his thumb fit into the curve; and that beautiful
clavicle. Like a spare rib from La Estrella. And her tits! She
looked like fucking Wonder Woman! He thought about the
night they got together, when she said, 'Let's go upstairs,'
and winked. That was ten months ago, at Goodbar's, the
bar across the street from Gristedes Brothers Grocers where
Arnie worked as a clerk, and at the cash register when they
were short a girl.

It bothered him a little that it had been Viv who initiated
their affair. It took a bit of the … *streak* out of it.

His cock was semi-hard.

Just the other day she explained it, by mistake. She told

him she never *ever* went home with a man who hit on her, because the one time she did 'after Tin Pan Alley' she was beaten up and raped and almost thrown off a roof. Carrie and Eli had been standing with them in the kitchen, eating Planters Dry Roasted Sunflower Seeds out of the glass jar in the shape of a peanut. Eli looked at the tops of his Converse and said, 'That's superstitious, though.' Carrie kept staring out the window at the lit-up windows and terraces of the McDonald's Building at the end of 71st. Munch munch munch.

Arnie closed his eyes again, and determinedly projected a succession of sexy scenes on the thirteen-foot ceiling above. Up on the cracked, slightly convex ceiling, through a filter of cigarette smoke, he watched ex-girlfriends getting it on. In white lace. But he couldn't stop coming back to the first night he met Viv. Dancing to the jukebox. Wearing a little t-shirt that said *Carnaby Street* on it in faded letters. She was playing the Beach Boys 'I Get Around' over and over and over and over. The same 45 floating, pausing for that pregnant second, then dropping, clicking into place. She had a belt of silver elephants, in a chain: trunk to tail, tail to trunk. Her tanned face tilted up to the low ceiling that was at the same level as the sidewalk (Goodbar's was a basement joint). Viv's eyes were closed and she was smiling her wide, slightly thin-lipped, crooked-toothed, very pretty smile. She slid into the wood booth next to him smelling of Charlie and sweat.

'I'm Viv Martian, can you believe it?' It really took him by surprise, her holding her hand out to shake like that, like a student council delegate.

Arnie said, 'How do you do, ma'am.'

But he already knew who she was. He'd noticed her his very first day at work. No bra on under her freebee Disco 92 T-shirt, with the matchstick thin, white-haired Carrie beside her, flipping through the Weekly World News, giggling to herself. On the rubber conveyer: three Hungry Man TV dinners, a can of Alpo, a can of El Bustello, and a Fosters oilcan. In spite of their shopping he thought they were rich, but the

17

check she wrote bounced, and his manager had him pin it to the board with an X through it. The next time they came in he pointed to it and smiled and asked her to pay cash. The conveyer was crowded. She told Carrie, 'Put it all back.' She kept a quart of milk and quart of Tropicana.

Viv was nothing like his Black Labrador-breeding suburban parents, and after the first night he moved on in – to this one-bedroom, where they all were now. Viv, Eli, Carrie, the mongrel Nora (half Doberman, half Cocker Spaniel), the old Burmese cat Fabian, a parakeet and two tortoises that lived behind the stove that Eli insisted survived on roach larva. 'They would not be alive! They would not be alive on so little Alpo.' That was only six months ago. God, it seemed like forever.

The pitter-patter of little snow-white feet.

A long, guttural, horror-movie style retch.

The earthy sound of the porcelain toilet seat slamming down. He took his hand out of his Jockeys and sat up. 'Carrie?'

'Yeah?'

'You ok?'

'Yeah.'

'Why aren't you at school?'

Another series of Exorcist-like retchings, then silence. He had not noticed, till that moment, the incredibly still air today. Very bright and very still out the courtyard window. The air was the temperature of water from the cold tap the moment you turn it on. Not cold. Not warm. Nada. 'You puking?'

'Yup-urguuchhhhh.'

The parakeet, Pathetic Nermal – had he really been chirping so merrily all along? He was belting it out from his cage in the kitchen. Imagine how tiny his ribcage must be. Arnie sat up and picked a roach out of the glass Playboy ashtray that was on the arm of the loveseat and lit it with his Zippo lighter, singeing his thumb. Then he paced around, pulled-as-he-turned the stiff knob on the TV, and watched the black and white eye open on him. He had to be back at Gristedes in two hours.

'Blueuarcccck.'

Stock duty. The best. Glenn, the meat guy, always had a ton of coke under Gristedes. The volume was down on the television. *The Price is Right* was on. A member of the audience was called and she jumped up and down and her tits were so big they smacked her in the chin. Arnie watched the screen and sang a song; he had a low, melodic voice. Under Gristedes, out of the sun. *Under Gristedes. People walking above. Under Gristedes, Gristedes.*

Carrie hugged the toilet, her cheek on the cool seat, her bare legs splayed on the checks of yellow and white on the pre-war floor. When the vomiting subsided, she recommenced worrying about the spelling quiz she'd studied so hard for and had missed – indeed had slept through – at ten that morning. She eyed several clods of toilet paper Eli and his friend Dylan had thrown on the ceiling last Easter, graying, collecting dust in their fissures, like little brains. Seven of them. One of these days she was going to stand up with a broom handle and knock them off. She listened to Arnie sing, and then he started coughing. She heard him pace around, get Nora's leash off the doorknob of the closet, try to find a dogshitbag in the kitchen cupboards; then she heard the heavy fireproof door to the apartment shut with barely a sound.

She came out in her I LOVE NY T-shirt and ran to the door and locked it. Then she ran and sat on the loveseat. Got up. Ran to the door again – her hair and nightshirt a red and black bleed as she darted past the mirror – and unlocked it, and ran, and sat, locked and ran and sat. She'd do it twenty times. CLACK *pitter patter* thump, *pitter patter* CLACK *pitter patter* thump, *pitter patter* CLACK. Getting a high grade on a make-up test: it smacked of cheating. It practically *was* cheating. She'd have an extra day to study – but by god she wasn't gonna use it!

After seventeen lengths she was back on the couch, panting. She picked up a Coke can with only Arnie's backwash in it, swooshed it in her mouth, and turned the TV volume up in time to hear the introduction, the lushly, soothing voice announcing the beginning of her favorite soap: *Like sands through the hourglass, so are the Days of Our Lives.* It looked like the best storyline was going to figure prominently: superb! The priest is actually Rod, the guy whose car sank during the summer, the swashbuckler, but he had had *amnesia.* Whether he was faking it or not remained to be seen …

The air smacked Arnie's face. It was almost cool now. It was going to rain. Fall was riding into the city like the Lone Ranger. Arnie whistled the William Tell Overture. He crossed Seventy-Second, threw a glance at Gristedes (there was no one in front), then took in his neighborhood (he liked having a neighborhood), a small dry cleaners, and above it, the psychic Miss Rosa's – her neon rose was lit all day – on the corner, was the Superette, where he decided he'd pop in for a quick Rolling Rock.

'You got ID, babycakes?' asked the wife of the owner. She was about fifty, wearing bright orange lipstick, and a black and white polka dot housedress. Eli called her Divine.

Arnie shrugged and winced, 'Come on. No.'

'You got anything else for me, maybe we could go in the bathroom for a minute, cutie?'

'Sorry.'

And back out again. Holding his arms across his chest as he was pulled by Nora, who always pulled on the same fucking southwesterly slant. He pulled back. Why they couldn't train this dog … He'd grown up with dogs, all wonderful, nothing like this. Arnie walked down the hill, under the big, gray, fast-moving cloud that he could see the beginning but not the end of, like a glacier in the sky. He passed the Mosque where he heard the sound of a hundred shoeless taxi drivers bowing. He headed across and over the ripped lawns at the entrance to Riverside Park, across the sandy patches, and past the swell of the little inaccessible hill, thick with six-foot tall weeds, the southern tip of Riverside Park with its big window of New Jersey. Further down he walked to the lower level, through a bouncy flap in a ripped steel fence and past a homeless colony – old bed sheets and umbrellas as roofs; coats as hats; men as women – under an unfinished overhang of the West Side Highway. He passed among them, they ignored him, and then he caught view of and approached Faggot Dock. Drinking his fucking Dr. Pepper. Passing barely anyone, just a fat middle-aged lady, tethered to an Akita with bad hip dysplasia (they're overbred). He headed through the tunnel and came out and down the hill; he still saw *no one*. Maybe there was a sale at Bloomingdales.

Ah! Phew! Here they all were, just beyond the ridge. There must have been fifty gay guys on and near the dock, even with the change in the weather, supine in their tiny Speedos, some in twos but mostly single, 'sunning' themselves. Nora's leash tinkled beside him. A choke-chain, of which he disapproved. Arnie walked with loose limbs and held the gold corduroy jacket his mother had bought at Sears tight around his chest with his free hand. He smoked with no hands. The five or ten guys sprinkling the lawn leading up to the dock (right by a tiny delicate cherry, already leafless); those who happened to be reapplying Ban de Soleil or looking for matches, or Marlboro Lights, or taking sips of Orangina or Manhattan Special Coffee Sodas, let their eyes linger. He was the David Cassidy type. One or two looked very easy, but he had Nora with him, and hadn't had anything to drink, and there was the roach, and Carrie's barfing. Viv said he was very sensitive. Viv said he was dyslexic. She said her father was quick, like him, but she was convinced he was dyslexic because he only read the sports page and the funnies. *DYSLEXIC*. He said out loud as he looked at the flesh-colored high rises of Fort Lee.

Or maybe Arnie was just stupid? I don't know. What do you think?

But this guy – he was at the edge of the pier – had been lying down then stood, gave the eye, so Arnie followed, dragging Nora, back down around by the baseball diamond. There was a concrete wall behind it, another piece of the unfinished overhang; it afforded privacy. Arnie undid his pants and the guy took off his glasses and knelt down. Arnie moved his dick in and out of the Hispanic guy's mouth, mumbling, 'Oh, baby. Oh, yeah.' Nora jumped and barked at Arnie's moving ass. After three minutes Arnie had to stop. Nora dragged him to the pier, pulling determinedly towards Jersey.

If you want to gaze on the miniature of Fort Lee, and its high-rises and the tiered roads cut into the Palisades, if you want to mark the progress of miniature buses and trucks, like that model on 'Mr Rogers' Neighborhood' when they drive into the Land of Make-Believe … you'd better be careful where you step, if you walk on the pier, because there are rotting planks and gaping holes. It even has signs on it, CONDEMNED. It was a work pier, for loading and unloading, originally, like in *On the Waterfront*. Except it's 1982, and you couldn't *pay* someone to buy NY. The sky was now darker, deep grey and dense as a shark's skin. Nora was smelling Lay's Chips, Hawaiian Tropic suntan lotion, the coming rain, her fellow dogs. All these, plus the alarm of the blowjob, had upset her delicate mutt balance. She lost her footing and dropped through a wide opening; her neck snapped in the choke collar.

Arnie knelt and shoved his arm through the mouth of 150-year-old splintered wood and scooped her hot middle into the cradle of his arm. Her black eyes bulged. Her tongue hung out, and her neck seemed too long. Was it? He held her body to his ear. He shook her, then took the Dr. Pepper out of his pocket and tipped it gingerly into her muzzle while rubbing her throat. He said, 'Come on. Come on, baby. '

She sputtered.

Her tongue slid back into her mouth.

She whimpered.

He sat there, stroking her in his lap, at the end of Faggot Dock. It started to rain. Big drops of cold rain.

After ten minutes, soaked, when they turned around to go home, there were no guys left on the pier, and the sight of the Upper West Side, rising up grey from the river, *was* from the other point of view.

2. 'Trouble', from *The Music Man*

WHAT WOULD *SHE* look like from the other point of view?
Viv wondered. It was the next night, and she stood in her
dark kitchen looking out the window at the lights in the
thirty-storey MacDonald's Building. She could see the blue-
and-mercury flicker of the evening news in one of them. Did
the fella over there watch her? She was singing 'Trouble',
from the 50s musical *The Music Man*. She danced three steps
into the living room where she circled around the little bit
of wood that was left exposed in the center of the cluttered
floor. Having finished with the part she could remember,
she nudged Eli, who was sitting at the table reading a book.
She started again from the top:

'*Are you Mr Dunlop?*'

Eli rolled his eyes.

She nudged him harder and whisked her hand, as in, *come
on*. 'I said: *are you Mr Dunlop?*'

Eli acquiesced. '*Yeah?*' In the singsong tone.

Viv continued. '*Well, either you're closing your eyes to a situation you do not wish to acknowledge or you are not aware of the
caliber of disaster indicated by the presence of a pool table in your
community.*'

'*Ma, I'm begging you, shut the fuck up.*' He used the singsong
tone for the ad-lib too.

'*Welllllll, you got trouble my friend. You got trouble right here
in River City. Well sure I'm a billiard player…*'

She had to skip some bits she couldn't remember.

'*The hours I spend with a cue in my hand are golden. I can see
you're the right kind of parents. I'm going to be perfectly frank.
First, medicinal wine from a teaspoon, then beer from a bottle!*'

Viv clapped, pirouetted, then went on:

'Mothers of River City – watch for the telltale signs of corruption: the minute your son leaves the house does he re-buckle his knickerbockers below the knee? Is there a nicotine stain on his index finger?'

Eli gave her the finger, pounded the table and yelled 'FUCK!'

'Jeez!' But she shut up. Eli didn't care that she had been the most famous director at Vassar in 1962, and she was glad of that. Viv liked the stakes *nonexistent*. She went back to the kitchen window. She wondered if there was any way she could determine which network the guy opposite had on. Would she need to study many televisions, in the dusk, from great distances, or could she intuit it? It didn't matter what you mastered, she thought. Why, you could master anything. What people think is valuable or worth learning is arbitrary. She picked a nearly unsmoked joint out of an ashtray on the windowsill, and lit it on the stove. She dragged, and kept looking out the window. The guy who lived in that apartment, with the terrace and the river view, on the 18th floor (what sunsets he must see!) he probably had a glass-fronted bookcase with monogrammed highball glasses, a glass-topped coffee table, those great leather-strip chairs from the Museum of Modern Art, framed Japanese silk prints on the wall. On his terrace there was a trellis, and on the trellis – she knew, because she watched him in the summer too – a thriving clematis. He lay out there all weekend, on a deck chair, very tanned, drinking out of a tall glass.

'Eli, you know what I wonder?'

'I'm trying to watch this.' There was a rerun of *The Loveboat* on the soundless TV. A couple were standing on the deck in evening dress, arguing. The woman stormed off, her gown trailing behind her. Eli was also reading, the thick silver paperback of *The Shining*. He had his orange-headphoned new Walkman on playing The Clash, 'Know Your Rights'. He sang along and took a huge bite of the second-to-last mini-slice of his Celeste Pizza With Everything For One.

His mom took a long drag on her joint, then put it down on the contact paper on the window ledge. 'Know Miss Rosa? The palm reader above the smaller dry cleaners? The one … the one … opposite the big one?'

'I'm watching this.'

Viv walked over to the TV and lit a tiny roach she picked out of the Playboy ashtray on top of it. She inhaled with her whole throat, and sucked the roach in by mistake. She spat the burnt paper wad, the size of a spitball, into her palm, then moved her tongue around in her mouth to clear the soot. She felt like some goofy animal in a cartoon.

'Where is Arnie anyway? Friday night, eight o'clock.' Eli put his finger to a nonexistent watch. 'His shift is over. We've gotta leave by ten to get front row. Where *is* he? Where's Carrie? Where is *everyone*?' He picked up his pizza crust and threw it on the floor for Nora. Eli grabbed her once she got it, and held her snout shut and waved her from side to side. She whined in her throat, then Eli pushed her away. Her long nails clattered as she slid noisily backwards on the blackened wood floor. Nora was having trouble getting the crust off the roof of her mouth, and gagged and opened her jaws wide.

'Carrie's at Helena's. Helena and Ralph took her out for dinner for her B'day, and then they were going to circle Manhattan on his yacht.'

'I though she was sick? You let her stay home from school.'

'She was sick yesterday. She said she felt better. Anyway it's her birthday.'

The thought of Carrie off yachting on her eleventh birthday left a faraway look in her mother's too-small eyes. There was a commercial on the TV, for Calgon bubble bath. A harried housewife wearing false eyelashes slips under the bubbles with her hair in a rolled-up towel, and the voiceover goes, *Calgon Take Me Away*. Even though the volume was turned all the way down Eli and Viv looked at the screen and heard it clearly.

Eight minutes later, eating from a small tub of Breakstones pineapple cottage cheese that expired today, thinking about whether to consult 'Miss Rosa' around the corner, and feeling nervous and now annoyed with herself for even considering going to a psychic Viv saw the door pushed opened. The little door-locker had returned early.

'What are you doing here?'

Carrie sat down at the table and put her pleather briefcase – what she thought of as her *attaché case*, but was actually an old backgammon case – down beside her, upright on the table. She had her red satin baseball jacket snapped up to under her chin. She took the last sip of Tropicana from a plastic cup – they only used picnicware; less dishes – and looked up at her beloved mother. The thick purple strap of a leotard showed under Viv's t-shirt; when Viv started wearing leotards under her t-shirts, it was officially fall. Eli was now in his closet-like, windowless room watching reruns of *The Honeymooners*. He had the sound up loud on his TV. On the living room TV barely-black anchorwoman Sue Simmons silently delivered a human interest story. First Sue Simmons stood in front of a hospital curtain, which was then pulled aside to reveal someone in a hospital bed. The laugher from *The Honeymooners* was raucous.

'That's a very loud laugh track,' Carrie yelled to Eli's room.

'It's not a laugh track. It was live. They shot everything live in the 50s.' said Viv, walking back to the kitchen window where she found the joint she left earlier had burned a hole in the black-and-white checked contact paper. She took a drag. It had gone out. She stood in the kitchen and addressed her daughter.

'You know 'takes a licking and keeps on ticking' – the Timex commercial? Even the commercials were live in those days, and they had this diver, all suited up, and he jumps

27

into the pool, a hi-dive' – here Viv had come to stand in the empty spot on the living room floorboards again, where she enacted most of the movements she described – 'and he swims to the end and climbs out again, right? And is supposed to tap his watch at this point' – she tapped her wrist – 'and says *takes a licking and keeps on ticking,* and they zoom in on the watch. Of course it wasn't ticking. Close up of a still second hand. But he said it *anyway*. He didn't handle the situation gracefully. He could have made it funny. You're not gonna even tell me what happened?'

'Helena got upset about some bullshit. She and Ralph had a fight before we were even on the BQE on the way to the Club, so we all came home. We dropped Helena at her mom's. He drove me home. I said I could walk.'

'In the Merc or the convertible?'

'It's a Merc convertible. Can you believe what he said to me, though? He said – you're gonna be one *hot number* when you grow up. I told him it was sexist but he said it wasn't. Where's Arnie?'

'I dunno if that's exactly sexist. Ok, yeah; yeah kinda. But he's a nice guy, don't ya think? Ralph would never try anything funny, do ya think? You have a very good sense of people.'

At the commercial, Eli positioned himself in the doorway to the living room. 'Where's fucking Arnie? We're going to the Shy-*ning*. We've gotta get there by ten or it'll be sold *out*. You are *not* coming.'

'?'

'Because, you always fuckin' cry 'n' shit.' He held his hands over his eyes, then cracked them: 'What's happening? What's ha- ha- happening? I ca- ca- ca- can't look!'

Carrie got up and headed to her room. She was closing the door behind her as Eli pushed it open. She flicked the light, and the Country Time Lemonade-yellow walls were blinding. The two black, almost ceiling-high windows that faced the courtyard were like missing teeth. Most people act differently in front of their back windows, let their hair down and whatever else out, when they think no one's watching. Carrie had a view of many old couples who tended to walk around in bucket-like underpants.

Eli knocked some stuffed animals and books off the shelf by the window with a swipe of his forearm and sat down. Carrie looked at him disgustedly. His white sweatsocks were pulled up to just below his hairless, gummy knees. The only other things he had on were a pair of cobalt-blue Fruit of the Looms and a too-small Devo t-shirt that someone had given him for his tenth birthday. The letters were stretched and peeling and impossible to make out.

She looked at the shelf. 'It'll break.' She stomped on a silverfish that slithered at superhero speed from under her bed. 'Got ya ya fuck.'

Eli bounced up and down on the shelf. It creaked, not wanting to break.

'Where does Helena get her dresses, Omar the Tent Maker? What does that fat bitch have to say for herself?'

'What do you mean, *have to say for herself*? Pretentious fuck.'

'What happened to *sailing takes me away*?' He sang the Christopher Cross song. Eli had a great voice; it hadn't changed yet; he was still in the Harlem Boys Choir.

'Helena had a titty attack about her dad's new girlfriend. But probably she was also jealous that it's my birthday. Her dad got me this Casio watch. It has a calculator. Like it? Ma! Tell Eli to get the fuck outta my room!'

He bounced up and down. *Creak-creak. Creak-creak.* 'Not until you tell me what the fight was about. I wanna play-by-play. You owe me that.' Eli picked up a rubber band, pulled it over the tip of his index finger and around the back of his thumb like a gun, then moved his fingers up and down, up and down. *Creak-creak.* He sang to the melody of Dona Nobis Pacem: '*What, was. The, fight. The fuck aboww oww out?*'

Five minutes later the shelf was split, but not without having left a giant yellow splinter in Eli's 'right ass'. Carrie's puny wrist had almost snapped during a passionately administered rope burn, and she now had Hubba Bubba in her hair.

The gum was stuck at the roots just above the left ear. She was going down the list of ways to avoid having to cut the whole watermelon-flavored gob out, again: nail polish remover, rubbing alcohol, turpentine. She sidled up to Viv and Arnie, who were standing at the kitchen window, and asked what they thought would do the trick. More than one person in the McDonald's building was watching them. None with much interest.

'No no no no – those will ruin the lovely color of your hair, dear. Remember, it went kinda *green*.' Viv said, as she ran her tongue over her teeth, wondering where they were. *Gone?* No: they were just numb from the coke Arnie had brought from Glenn under Gristedes.

'Well, I have a patch here – and here – already, and it's starting to look like they do experiments on me.' She held long flaps of hair up to expose a peachfuzz bald spot above her other ear, and one at the nape of her neck.

Carrie was interrupting one of the most substantial conversations Viv thought she and Arnie had ever had. The coke made them *muy serioso*, as they stood backlit at the window. Viv felt their shapes must look extremely sexy, seen from the block cubes of lit rooms and shadowy terraces of the McDonald's building. Arnie was adding to that impression – unbeknownst to Viv – by dint of having recently had one of the best blow jobs of his short life in an apartment on the 18th floor. At the moment Carrie arrived (she still had the satin jacket on, like she'd forgotten her cue), they were in front of a ridged, clam-shaped fake tortoiseshell Maybelline compact with two large – *respectable*, even – lines of coke cut out on it.

They had heard Eli's singing and Carrie's yelping through

the window, through the courtyard; the courtyard air is a 'high messenger.' But Viv had pinched Arnie's shoulder saying, 'Let them work it out. It's good for them.' Now Carrie appeared, at the level of his lower ribs and her mother's upper tits.

'I'm coming to the fucking movie.'

Arnie patted her head, 'You'll freak, baby.'

'Don't call her *baby*. We're gonna have to cut it out, sweetheart.' Viv pulled scissors from a tin can covered in felt (a relic from the William T. Sherman School Crafts Fair two years back, in Eli's 'Darth Vader Period') and tipped Carrie forward over the slot where the dishwasher used to be. Carrie's colorless hair dropped into one of the cokelines on the mirror. Arnie lifted it between his thumb and index fingers, like he was plucking a dandelion for wish-blowing.

Viv was quietly snipping as little hair as she could. 'Remember after *Carrie*, Carrie? You had to sleep with me for a week. I think *The Shining* will just scare the living shit outta you, sweetheart. A woman actually dropped *dead* at a showing of *The Shining*. It was the headline of the Post, remember? *THE DIE-NING*?'

'You can die of fear. It's true. I saw it on *In Search Of*. But that wasn't the reason I slept with you. It was because your mother died.'

'No it wasn't, honey. You never even met my mother.'

'Your mom died. We saw *Carrie*. We got Nora from the pound. All on the same *day*. How can you say what caused the nightmares?'

'*That* was a mistake.' Viv said enigmatically. 'Straight out to the pound. Obviously trying to replace something. Even though you never met my mom – I don't know, I guess it's true, the psychic absence.' She looked up from the snipping, unused to going uninterrupted for so long. She licked her absent teeth and tried to explain again: 'We might have waited, saved up for a *quality pet*.' This to Arnie, because he complained from time to time about Nora – that her head

31

was too small, her neuroses. Arnie was looking out the window, rolling a roach in his fingers, wondering if she really was fucking nuts. Eli insisted she was. Eli said 'Mom's off her rocker.'

While Viv continued making tiny snips at the two-inch patch of hair she was removing, Carrie told Arnie, 'I had these nightmares – about Rhinebeck, about Grandma and Grandpa's house. I was in their Volvo, with Helena, going for the weekend – and when we turned up the driveway all the lights were on already. The windows were bigger, like big owl's eyes. No one was supposed to be home, so we were worried there was a burglar and we went around the back…' As she narrated Carrie saw the sneakers with laces tied together, the ones high school kids threw over the telephone poles above the junction at the foot of her grandparent's driveway, and she saw the black swervy marks their drunk wheels left on the road, right under the sneakers. Her grandparent's road was called Pumpkin Lane, a name Carrie would have liked, in her school-girly aspect, under any other circumstances; a name she would have liked in a book, had she not hated it in Rhinebeck. She felt like crying now, because she saw the bored looks on Arnie and her mother's faces. She wished she had never started telling about the dream. She stopped. Viv had given up with the hair and was kissing Arnie's neck. Arnie was looking down at Carrie. Carrie would not finish describing the nightmare, and the dead kid in it with a body light as styrofoam, which was the coolest part. She looked back at Arnie. Nice to have a face you can't read around the house. Nice to have a man around the house.

Carrie *chassé-d* across the room, tried to *temps levé* a silverfish and missed it, then removed the heavy plastic top of the record player which sat on a sagging upside-down wicker basket. She put on big headphones that covered both sides of her face, pulled a crocheted blanket over her head, and saw only the red, blue and tan stitches made by some dead relative of another era. *There Goes Rhymin' Simon* was on the turntable, spinning silently. Carrie flicked on the heavy lever of the amp. She listened and stared at the yarn from so close up she was able to induce a calming hallucination. A little scene with hills and dancers and clouds.

Meanwhile at the window, Viv put her hand on Arnie's dick, feeling the heat come through it. Viv said, 'Take her? She really wants to come.' Then snorted her last line. Arnie was about to get around to telling Viv to control Eli a bit. For Eli's sake. He was going to say he would take Carrie, *if* Viv would promise to smack the shit out of Eli the next time; but as usual Viv beat Arnie to the mike. This time she divulged something she regretted – vaguely, but deeply – the next time they fucked, later that night:

'I know this might be hard to believe', she whispered loudly, gesturing towards the rocking lump under the crocheted throw, 'but I think about – I guess you could call them *checks and balances of power*.' She took Arnie's Merit and dragged an expressive J. Edgar Hooverish drag, with the image of J. Edgar Hoover in women's lingerie in her head. 'I let Carrie win with me. I try to show her that she will *always* win. And therefore, she will.' The smoke came out in an oozing gust and Arnie liked her little wet, shiny white, crooked teeth.

He put his face up next to the cat screen in the window and counted, moving his lips, up to the eighteenth floor of the McDonald's Building, then he took five straight gulps of his Rolling Rock before shouting at the top of his lungs: 'POWER TO THE PEOPLE! POWER TO THE MOTHER-FUCKING-COCKSUCKING-PEOPLE!'

'Shut up or you'll get us all thrown out!' There had been numerous complaints about them from semi-naked elderly neighbors.

When Carrie, Eli and Arnie set off about 10:45 walking to 56th, garbage was blowing high in the air over wide, empty crosswalks. They were forty-five minutes off schedule, by Eli's estimate. He had been wanting to see this movie for *two years*, and it had *finally* been re-released, for midnight show-ings only. *Why* Viv had not let him see it when he was ten, when it first came out, in 1980, he would never understand. He'd seen *everything*.

Coked-up Viv, left alone and glad to be, conceived at the window that she loved Arnie. He had taken her children out to a horror movie, at midnight. They were safe with him. And they did love him. The psychic, she'd talk to her. Something about the psychic was calling to her. Like a pretty plastic bead you might find on the floor while you're vacu-uming and that you hold in your hand until you finish – and amuse yourself by daydreaming about searching – searching through the city, through other boroughs and on into New Jersey, if necessary – for beads just like it, to make a neck-lace. But when you're done, you've accumulated lots of other crap: bobby pins, bits of cat food, shreds of old socks, and you end up throwing the bead away. Not by accident, but because by then you know you'll never do anything with it.

Still.

Viv counted out thirty-two quarters from an El Bustello can and headed out to see Miss Rosa above the smaller dry cleaners.

3. cihcysP

VIV STOOD ON top of the smaller dry cleaners, in the center
of the old ballroom, eight quarters in each hand and eight
in each Levis' front pocket. She was aware of the bulges in
her pockets and the sweat in her palms, in the wrong way;
they felt like new parts of her body. Miss Rosa was watching her, still as an owl. The psychic's hair was pulled up in a
pink terry-cloth turban, with a shiny copper broach holding
it together in the front. She had a black widow's peak; two
strands of hair were twisted and stuck to either side of her
face in big Cs. Her green sunken eyes were arced in metallic
green shadow, and outlined in black kohl. On her cheekbones snaked half a dozen moles which Viv was certain were
fake. On the frail rails of her wrists, rainbow bangles with
bits of glass and sequins jangled. Her black velvet dress had
bucket sleeves, and was coated with a spidery mesh of orange lint. She sat at a large round table draped in a deep red
tablecloth, in front of a ceiling-height plate-glass window
and under a buzzing neon rose. She rested her thin hands,
with their giant knuckles, on her crystal ball, which was not
quite as large as it ought to have been. The smoke from her
long True Blue 100 cigarette sailed up to the ceiling rose.

Miss Rosa eyed the elephants on Viv's belt and coughed
out, 'Republican? That's the GOP symbol ya know. The
elephant.' Her powdered nostrils flared.

'God no. I'm very liberal.'

'Abortion not a moral no-no, then?' She stubbed out her
cigarette.

'How did you know I was pregnant?'

What was she doing here? Viv wondered. Had she come

to the psychic to *hear* she was pregnant? She had a sharp pain in her temple. She let her eyelids flutter shut. She stood breathing deeply in the center of the room.

This move struck Miss Rosa as surprisingly melodramatic. Here was an easy one: Viv bore the telltale signs of a pregnant, college-educated forty-year old at her wit's end. But the acting, the heavy breathing; that was a bit odd. Not your usual customer.

Viv repeated her question, 'How did you know?'

Without turning around she pointed to the word *Psychic* stenciled backwards on the window.

(The truth: Miss Rosa had not touched her tarot deck in seven years, hadn't read a palm in six, and now, even the inoffensively New Age-y *I Ching* was losing favor. The only service she offered involved looking into her crystal ball and talking.)

Viv felt stronger. Whenever Viv felt weak, and her eyes fluttered, and she did not know where or sometimes even who she was – she just buckled down, found her balance with her eyes closed, did some deep *ujai* breathing, and told herself: *she was Viv*. She opened her eyes and approached Miss Rosa, who seemed to shrink. Viv pulled out a chair, sat down, planted her feet wide and put her hands on her knees like a truck driver.

'Listen – this is going to sound … ' – she looked at the old lady and chose the wrong word – '… *dotty*, but all I really want to know is if there is something wrong with it. If I keep it, will it be sound? Because my kids … I've already got kids, and I don't think any of us could handle a retard.'

'I don't get the sense there is anything wrong with it.' She dragged on a new True Blue, and closed her eyes while Viv exhaled loudly, taking immense comfort from the fact that she was not carrying a retard. Her palpable relief gave the psychic pause. *This* was really the customer's question? This lady wanted to know if the embryo she was going to abort was sound.

'But how the hell would I know? There might be. There *might* be something wrong with it. It might be a hermaphrodite or something.' Miss Rosa smiled, and her eyes twinkled.

They sat for a few minutes in silence. The 'psychic' stared at her too-small crystal ball with undue attention, because she was embarrassed and confused by her outburst. She'd broken character. She'd been in character for six years – on the job, that is. And when she wasn't on the job she was alone; she was no one, she barely existed.

'Well, would it be? *Would* it be ok? Just try and see.' Viv stood over Miss Rosa and tapped the crown of the ball.

Miss Rosa held her little old lady/witch hand up, as if to say *Stop* – then brought it to rest on the globe – the crystal ball in which the future had never *exactly* appeared. The one she'd bought one evening in the early Fall of 1966. She shut her eyes and saw the elephants on Viv's belt; tail to trunk, trunk to tail. It reminded her of stitched piece, a 'circus scene' she'd executed for her mother a thousand years ago. After a moment she said, in a very low voice, a masculine voice, 'Lemme think about it. Lemme think about it. I'm thinking about this.'

She saw: Viv's face in 1966 when they met downstairs at Woolworth's. She remembered. Next she saw a sixteen-year-old boy's face, a face a fair bit like Elvis Presley's, a fair bit like the young Viv: tired, slightly greasy, sneering.

'It's a tadpole at the moment – not even animal; a bean. Fine though. As fine as a bean can be.'

Viv wondered if that *meant* anything. She was looking at Rosa's mantle: tacky tchotchkes (gifts from grateful clients). She looked at the floor, which was layered in small, dirty Persian rugs, then the hallway. A bulbous ochre lamp on a small bookcase. Viv looked at her own hands and then Miss Rosa's, who continued conversationally, 'What *you* do for a living?'

'I work at Macy's. I guess I just have to decide whether to keep it at this point.'

'*Here*? Blech. Send it elsewhere.'

'There *is* no elsewhere. This is this one's only chance. And it's not looking good for it. You should see the father.' Viv stood up next to the wall of window, breathed on it, wiped her own mist, and looked across the wide road to the other side of 72nd Street, to Gristedes' blue awning which was thin and full of holes with bits flapping. The other shops had black windows, but there were tall street lamps, and traffic signs swinging amber, and one reflection in a dark window of Miss Rosa's red rose sign glowing over the stenciled word *cihcysP*.

Viv vaguely wondered when it had stopped being night in the city. The thought of 'The City Never Sleeps' advertising campaign for some bank – she could not remember which – suddenly struck her as brilliant, symptomatic 'of the times', and sent a wave of excitement through her. And then suddenly she was so, so tired. Cocaine didn't peter out; coke *ducked* out, like a robber. She lowered herself down again opposite Miss Rosa, putting her hands first on the hard, over-stuffed arms of the tomato-like chair – the way a heavily pregnant woman would. She ran her tongue over her slimy little teeth as she said, 'He's not even twenty, the dad. He took the kids to the movies. Carrie, my daughter, she's eleven today, she was sick yesterday. Some bug, but she begged us to let her go to *The Shining*.' Then she started and stopped crying in under ten seconds. 'It's not so much the abortion as this is *my* last chance, the end of *my* purposefulness.'

'Ha! Come on. That's nonsense – *purposefulness*! Chance at what, lady? Come on. Buck up! Have a scotch. No charge.' She sprang up as she spoke, took a Prague red glass goblet from a set of six on the mantle, blew into it, coughed, walked over to the sink and rinsed it. 'I sleep on the sofa. It folds out, very comfy. Nice high ceilings, though. An old ballroom. Plus bath. Know how long I've lived here? Sixty-seven years.' Miss Rosa watched a medium-sized cockroach run across the sink.

Viv drank the Red Label in a shot. Rosa seemed a very nice lady. The booze warmed her throat and chest. She seemed a saint. 'You must have heard a lot of great stories, over the years.'

'You'd be surprised.'

Viv sat in the chair with her eyes closed and her finger-tips touching and her lips slightly puckered as she imagined herself buying a used Cadillac on layaway, driving to Jones beach (Beach 9, the surfer's beach) in the summers, living out her days without a man and no more kids. She was almost asleep but also thinking about the fact that she had worked in two places called The Self Center. One in college, during the summer break, a beauty parlor on Cape Cod – she could feel the ocean air coming through the open door and mixing with the smell of hairspray; she could hear the bells attached to the door, and the sound of the waves … And now this Health Food joke at Macy's where she spent most her days, alone, behind the counter eating expired sunflower seeds. What were the chances of that happening? Two places called The Self Center.

'The truth is my life has been … well, I don't know if you would call it *interesting…*' Miss Rosa began, and Viv woke up.

Motherfucker! Viv's eyes flew open. She hadn't seen this coming. (The truth is she hardly ever saw anything coming; she made things come, in a very small compass.) But she said nothing, and she climbed off her chair and knelt on a dirty little rug and looked up at the medium's dainty feet, feeling like the devotee at an ashram she'd just seen a picture of in *Time* magazine. Viv shifted her weight from her left to her right ass, then distributed it evenly betwixt the two, pulled her shoulders back, straightened her spine, took another long, deep, noisy *ujai* breathe, and glanced mourn-fully into her delicate, empty, red glass.

''Nother?' Miss Rosa was glowing in the red-amber light of her sign and the streetlamp. Viv was not sure. Booze, for a boring and probably fictitious life story? Miss Rosa still had a pretty face; she looked like Jean Rhys. OK! Yes! Viv was sixteen again, inspired, engaged, compassionate.

4. The Neon Rose

IT ALL ENDED when she was 16. No. First to explain the whole psychic mix-up, or charade, or smokescreen, or job, however you want to see it. From when she was 16 in 1915 until 1976, she had barely existed. She had no friends, no job. She shopped, she said hello to the check-out girls. She walked in the park, she said hello to the children. Once a week she saw a movie. That was it. She had her reasons. She will get to her reasons. But finally, due to lack of funds, at 77, in '76, she re-invented herself. Phoebe Curtis (that's who she really was) came up with Miss Rosa the day she found the neon rose – a glorious piece that should have cost a thousand bucks – for twenty at a garage sale in Princeton. She'd come to her profession, she explained, pretty much by chance. But, strangely, this chance had presented itself twice.

Viv, still at her feet, her eyes closed, said to Miss Rosa/ Phoebe Curtis, 'Arnie is from there! Arnie is from Princeton New Jersey!'

'You don't say.'

She was there, in Princeton, that day of the Bicentennial year, to get an old book, a vanity publisher's history of Rhinebeck. That was the town where she grew up. She hoped it would mention her family, her Aunt Hilda, and a little boy she once knew – her cousin. She'd seen the book advertised on the side of a page in the New Yorker. But when she got to the address, on a street near the edge of town – she found that the dealership had burnt down. It was all boarded up like something in a cartoon. There were slanting planks nailed over the broken glass door. She turned and walked back to her white Beetle, noticing that she was less dejected than she should have been. Maybe it was the sunny day? She stopped at a yard sale. There, she divined, a marriage had gone sour.

It was a perfect day, a clear bright day, like the day in a little souvenir of a beach. The sky was liquid turquoise above NJ. On a crew-cut lawn, on top of and under card tables, in topless cardboard boxes, half falling out like the entrails of roadkill and emitting a brownness only years in a basement can produce, lay the standard suburban impedimenta: cracked garden hoses, decade-old fashion mags, toasters, invalid trays, dumbbells, a punch set, sun loungers, a big wood-encased TV…

Both spouses were present, not speaking, dividing the cash. She had bleached hair, rosacea, and a cast on her arm. He: fresh sutures along his Brutus-like jaw. They were drinking Rolling Rocks from a bright yellow cooler with a sign on it that said *Not for Sale* in some kid's handwriting.

Viv said, eyes still closed, 'You know they do, they *really* do sound like his parents. He lived there.'

Phoebe said, 'Doubtful, though.'

Phoebe poked around, on, and under each of the tables. An older couple picked up a charming dollhouse for five dollars. It came with all the furniture. *Murray look how sweet! What a bargain!* Her problem, Phoebe explained, was that she was incapable of forgetting anything.

'Was he *really* called Murray? Those are the kids' fucking grandparents. They have a house in Rhinebeck and they antique in Princeton, and, and, they have a dollhouse I know they bought at a yard sale there. Carrie loves it. She's asked them for it about a hundred times and they always say no because *it isn't a toy, it's an antique.* Carrie imitates them.' Viv had opened her eyes and poured another shot with a shaky hand.

Phoebe took the bottle, and drank out of it while giving Viv a look, 'Christ knows … maybe they are. Maybe they're your ex-in-laws at your boyfriend's parents' yard sale. If it helps you to think of it that way, then think of it that way.'

Under a mountain of coiled, thick black cable … Phoebe just *knew* there was something for her. She crawled under a table, and rooted about. (She was 77 but felt just as she had at 35: 'not great'.) Finally, all the way back, a curve of dusty glass. She dragged the long cable onto the lawn, wiped the grime on the denim dress she'd be wearing for the next three years, and pulled gently at the glass nub.

It was the length of a five year-old, and it was shaped like one. When she first saw it – lying on its side there, one big leaf on the ground like a crooked elbow holding the head of the flower, the other arm crooked too, hand on waist, elbow in the air, another leaf. It was so beautiful. She could feel the young apprentice in her workshop, making him, at night. A neon artist. Phoebe could feel the *commitment* in the thing, as it lay there on the green grass, far from dead. She asked: 'What color does it light up?' Got no answer. And continued, louder, 'Hey lovebirds, how much for the rose?' 'Fitty,' said the man through an exhalation of cigar. The woman, or Arnie's mom, looked on. 'Twenny.' She said. 'I made it. It's red.'

Phoebe had a twenty. Literally her last. She grabbed the rose like a mannequin – slotted her arm over its waist, and tore off, though once in the car – with the end of its stem sticking out the back of the open hatchback – she took a quick glance in her rearview mirror. A chubby boy stood in an upstairs window. He was only *almost* hidden by the leafy elm branches that drooped over the whole sorry affair.

Phoebe noticed that Viv might be asleep and said, loudly, 'It was probably Arnie. I do remember the boy. I'm not making this up. His yellow hair.'

The reason she was out of dough was that two months before her monthly money had ceased to arrive at the post office box it'd been arriving at for 67 years. Her father, who sent the checks – because she told him if he didn't, she would tell her mother he was gay, which she also wasn't making up – must have died. She had been planning, screwing up

43

her nerve, figuring out what to say to the welfare office…
but suddenly it was all clear. She would go into business, be
a psychic. Miss Rosa. She already had that crystal ball. It'd
been providing balance in the toilet cistern for ten years, but
what was to stop her putting it to better use?

'Funny thing is I'd tried once before. I was almost a psychic once before. My first attempt was a total failure. But I'm
glad. I'm glad I failed because if I hadn't I would never have
met Lavender. He's the little boy I mentioned? Of course I
did – I was looking for *him* in the book. It's all about him.'

She was fifteen when she first left, first tried to get here;
from Rhinebeck to NYC. It was a town consensus: they wanted Phoebe Curtis out, which was kind of strange, because
she never, ever said a word. Maybe that was the problem.
The burghers, the lawyers and farmers, the church widows,
the teachers and the doctor put their heads together and
managed to get Phoebe a job as a lady's maid, at the Apthorp Hotel in Manhattan. Mrs Edgecomb and her daughter
would pay four dollars a week, which would be posted to
Rhinebeck, to Phoebe's relieved and grateful parents, Cotton and Lucretia Curtis.

Phoebe, at that time, believed herself in possession of a
true psychic gift.

'It's just observation. An observant nature, a lack of im-
agination, and the limited world I choose to come in contact
with. God, but then, *then* … I thought I was destined for
fame 'in the eyes of gods and men'. But it was not to be. Not
Nostradamus, nor was meant to be.' Miss Rosa took three
long swigs, with two gulps each, of Red Label.

On the top floor of the Apthorp, in front of a room in a row
of other maids' rooms, they chucked her trunk. She thought
her life was beginning; that this night was the beginning of
a great, indeed, an *historic* life. Everything was a sign. A *Saturday Evening Post* fluttered on her bare mattress, throwing
itself open to the gossip column.

Mr JIM TANQUERAY, DASHING TANQUERAY GIN HEIR, SEEKS A WIFE.

CAREFREE CLARETTA MAZE WALKS BAREFOOT DOWN FIFTH AVENUE.

Phoebe sat on the ledge, twelve stories up, lighting and relighting a half a corncob pipe she'd stolen from her father. On either side of West End, new townhouses faced each at irregular intervals, in very different styles, like chess pieces in an endgame. Further down the hill a threadbare slope dropped to the Hudson; across the river the Palisades rose like a high red hand. NYC was somehow *more empty* than Rhinebeck, though the river was wide and brimming with boats big and small, the streets with ladies and their maids, and men buying and selling things to each other. And horses, and horseshit. The blankness was the city's self-awareness, its self-consciousness, even. Which is weird, and as awful to consider as the thought of a child knowing it's being born. And why *shouldn't* it know?

The fifth of Red Label was now empty. Phoebe spun it, and it turned fast and silently on the red tablecloth.

All that evening, no one came. Not to say hello, not to offer dinner. She been instructed to unpack, but instead she just sat, staring out the window. It got dark, and the noises of Broadway were almost gone.

She tried to undress. Her mother Lucretia had always 'undone' her. She'd pull her daughter's hair and pinch her arms hard, then – ever so gently – fold the dress and lay it on the bedroom chair. But no matter how roughly Phoebe twisted and yanked and pulled her own tits, she couldn't get the corset and attached bloomers a third of the way off. There were hundreds of knots and bows she'd always assumed were decorative. After an hour she gave up, sweaty and crying, and lay down in bed with the thing still half-on. It made a sort of lumpy pillow from her shoulder to hip, a dead Siamese twin. Then she heard it.

She propped herself and her corset up on her elbow, and listened: laughing, slapping that sounded like a baker throwing bread, a self-conscious, high moan: this was what Cotton and Lucretia did not do! Did once, and forever paid the price for, as Lucretia put it. It was a sign! Phoebe closed her eyes and saw a giant's iron cauldron, a man and a woman's face, coming up and gasping then being tugged under. A big strong or a little salt-cracked hand, a foot, a bent knee with a loose stocking, rising and sinking.

Next morning, thinking herself supremely worldy-wise, she offered advice on what the younger Edgecomb should wear if she wanted Mr Jim Tanqueray to propose. They were at breakfast. The silver was excessive, and it looked like you needed to yell over it.

Phoebe screamed: a *green dress with a yellow bonnet!!!!!!*

Her instructions must be followed to a T! The Higher Power had sent her the sex noises of the couple next door and now she trusted her vision. She spoke of whatever came into her head.

Between breakfast and lunch, Phoebe was sent to the Apthrop Pharmacy three times for vials of cocaine; both the ladies Edgecomb were 'quite fond of it'. They snorted and plotted and chewed ice cubes and ate radishes with salt for lunch.

That evening, at the Opera, Mr Tanqueray proposed to Barefoot Claretta, and was overheard to say that a grown woman should never wear yellow. There was a row when the Younger Edgecomb got home. Phoebe had *known* that Tanqueray hated yellow! Phoebe was a witch! How else could she explain only putting vinegar on her meals. Meat, bread, veg. Vinegar, vinegar, vinegar!

The Elder Edgecomb actually wept, and shoving the final thimble-full of the evening up her slack nostril, said that although she'd wasted a great deal on having Phoebe shipped, she would have to be returned. It had been less than two days.

A rumpled clump of her corset protruded from the top of her dress as Phoebe rode through Rhinebeck, on the way home from Woodstock station, in the back of Farmer Morkam's gig. She'd changed. She sneered *openly*. It had taken her two days to learn what other people spend their lives *not* learning. Which is that you aren't who you'd like to be. No no no: you just fucking aren't.

Of course, she was in for it at home. Lucretia tied her daughter to the porch swing. She was to remain there overnight. This was a tradition, the tying-up. Phoebe was often tied to a post, or the sink, or sometimes to her bed. She sat facing a field from which Cotton and the farmhands had just taken the zucchini and the string beans. Their work left a chaotic ruin.

Lucretia tossed an unfinished cushion cover at her daughter, purple flowers in a blue vase. Berlin Work: stitch-by-numbers. Phoebe loathed them. The house overflowed with them. Some framed, some on cushions, affixed to curtains, used as placemats. Lucretia then threw several more at Phoebe's head. After the vase came an owl on a branch, for which it was far too large, then a heart with the words HOME IS WHERE THE HEART IS written in it. There was also a slimy mermaid in some distress on a rock, a fairy covered in smaller fairies that looked like gnats, and a hunky black man in shackles, the links of which cleverly spelled out ONE AND GOD MAKE A MAJORITY. Phoebe moaned aloud when she saw it. It was tiny and would take about ten years.

Phoebe climbed off her chair and violently shook Viv awake.

Viv looked at her like a happy toddler. She didn't know shit, but she was full of piss and vinegar.

Phoebe slurred, 'Ya know thing about owl, though: in the fifties I was at a Zoo, Bronx Zoo, and a birds-of-prey fellow explained how owls sit with perfect ease on the thinniest branches. An all along I'd thought ... whoever did the stencil for that disgusting scene would 'ave had *no* idea, would

47

'ave done *no* research, because it was such schlock. *That's* the funny thing.'

Viv was totally out of it, 'Sorry. Sorry I fell asleep. That's awful. How rude.'

'Go home! Sleep it off lady!' Phoebe smiled and slapped Viv's back.

Viv left.

Phoebe looked out the window at dark 72nd street, then crawled over and lay down on the sofa without opening it. She hadn't told anyone anything about herself since she arrived in NY for the second time, less than a year after the first.

5. Irene Cara's on the Ticket Holder's Line!

THIS WAS ELI's second time trying to get to a midnight show. On the way downtown he and Carrie got into a big argument about a plastic owl on a fire escape, about its purpose. The owl had a pigeon standing on its head. Carrie thought that ruled out Eli's assertion that it was a pigeon deterrent.

Carrie said, 'Deterrent: stops something from happening.'

Eli pulled her hair down to his hip and made her walk that way for a block, saying, 'You don't like this much, huh? This is a deterrent for no more of your lip. Deterrent. Deterrent. *Deterrent.*'

Passing the grubby tubular Coliseum, Arnie saw some guys he knew standing in the dry fountain at Columbus Circle. Arnie nudged the clump of kid and jaywalked. 'Stop acting like retards.'

A crowd of about fifty 'hippies' were strewn around, inside, and along the rim of the fountain. There was a woman nursing a toddler; someone in shades lying flat with their hands in prayer; a couple making out; a shirtless guy wearing a rainbow afro. That was Arnie's old friend, Whirly.

As they approached, Arnie called 'Howdy Partner.'

Whirly said 'You had kids fast.'

Whirly reached slowly into his cut-offs' pocket, then shook Arnie's hand, and winked. He said 'Have a nice ride, pop' and gestured in the direction they had been walking. They set off.

Eli said, 'That was weird.' And then, 'Man – you met more people in high school than most people do their whole lives.' Arnie *did* seem to know everyone. Or *almost* know them.

Arnie looked into his palm, wondering what drug Whirly

had put there. A Superman tab. His cape flung out from his blue-muscled shoulders, one leg bent, the other straight: he was taking off. He was taking a flying leap. A large tab of acid, about an inch long. A *huge* tab of acid. Arnie put it on his tongue.

Horrifyingly, the ticket buyer's line began four blocks uptown from the Ziegfield; it turned the corner of 54th, and headed up Sixth Avenue.

Eli was instantly hysterical. 'That *can't* be it. That can't be for *The Shining*. We still have 45 minutes. I fucking told you! We should *not* have stopped.'

Carrie was right behind him.

Arnie was last, feeling like a movie star on the red carpet, with a carwash of eyes going past. Eli, Carrie, Arnie; a strange trio, at half-past-eleven on a crisp NY night. One woman returned Arnie's optimism. She was *gorgeous*, like Irene Cara, rainbow beads quietly clattering at the tip-ends of soft ginger-coloured cornrows. The rest of the crowd blurred. She emitted a sexy, you're-with-the-kids smile. Arnie slowed, and panned back with his best – Clean and American and Young, baby.

Arnie called to Eli, 'Don't get your panties in a wad.'

Eli screamed over fifty feet, for ten times that many people to hear: 'If we hadn't have stopped to talk to your *fucking acid freak friend*!'

Irene Cara, whose name was Lucy, watched them walk on. These were the kind of interesting people she wanted to meet. Maybe. Actually, what kind of people *were* they? She'd been in New York less than a year, up from Atlanta.

'Take a chill pill!' Carrie called quietly to Eli. About thirty people could hear her.

Eli pivoted, smacked Carrie upside the head and her chin snapped forward. She used its momentum to speed up and past him, aiming to avoid another blow. Eli stuck the top of his Adidas under her escaping Puma, and lifted it. She fell on her knees. There were layers of people between the line and the little scene. Arnie had missed the first half of the move, having turned back to look at Lucy. Arnie shot a wholly inappropriate faceful of old-fashioned possibilities her way before noticing her worried expression, as she looked past him. He turned back to the kids, grabbed the back of Eli's curly black head, rocked him onto the balls of his feet and shook him. 'Fucking *stop*. What are you gonna be – a fucking *murderer* when you grow up?'

Loosed, Eli ran ahead and threw open the door into the red lobby. It was freezing cold; the air conditioners were on. Inside a glass box beside the ¾-life-size ceramic rendering of Ben Hur's elephants, framed by an art deco oblong copper bevel, stood a girl with a polyester white-and-black pinafore and a Long Island accent. She was writing out, very- fucking- slowly, the Sold Out sign. Inside her booth the fumes of permanent marker were almost unbearable, and she felt like she might faint.

Eli thrust his forehead flat against the glass when he saw it. '*Owwww*. Fuck this!' He left a greasy smudge she was powerless to remove.

'I'll call the manager if you use that kind of language in here,' she gasped into her microphone, the zircon cross on her neck glittering.

They stood in front of the uncanny elephants, saying nothing. They slumped out the door and stood in front of the smug ticket-holders' line. Eli held his fingers in the shape of guns and moved them up and down at Arnie's chest.

'If you hadn't have stopped. If you *hadn't* have stopped to talk to that acid freak. Fuck shit piss ass.'

Carrie said, 'We could see something else. We could go to *Rocky Horror*?' She was still at the stage of trying to figure out what people want. Though it wasn't long before she'd realize that people don't want you to give them what they want, unless you pretend you don't *know* what they want. Very boring.

'Let's get the Post.' Arnie of the Conciliatory Gesture. Because they'd need to pass Irene Cara on the heavenly ticket-holders' line again. Arnie felt his limbs loosening. Trails? He ran his open-fingered hand in front of his eyes: *pink* trails.

'I'm having visuals. I'm having hallucinations.' He raised a finger like a teacher. 'But that is OK, class.'

Carrie said 'What?' looking up at him. Her face. It was still her face. Certainly, absolutely. But also a pansy from his mom's NJ garden, the ones in the border right by the gate, all pulled in at the center and all light at the sides. Afternoons with absolutely nothing to do at his ma's kitchen table. Plates of Fig Newtons. *Welcome Back Kotter, Hustlers*.

'What are *trails*?' Carrie's eyes darted over him, a slow pinball on the subtle incline of the deck. What was she looking at? She came and held his hand. She was a perfect girl. A flower. Meanwhile other people's faces were made of raw chicken parts, like the ones he packed in styrofoam and plastic wrap under Gristedes. Booze was called for; he *hated* tripping. Why did he always fucking forget that? He snorted out loud at the thought.

On Fifth they stuck a quarter in a newspaper dispenser and Eli took out the last three Posts, just to be a dick. Further along the sidewalk the tail end of the snake of admirers began to move steadily into the mouth – no – door of the Ziegfield. Though it had teeth. And purple lips. In great fear and profound agitation, Arnie wrote Gristedes's number on a ripped-off piece of the corner of the Post, left the kids, and ran back to the line. He found her. Irene Cara. Talking to her girlfriend as if nothing depended on anything else. Arnie ran up and touched her elbow. She jumped. 'Lord God!'

'This is my number. Use it.'

He jogged back to where the kids had sat themselves down on some wide church steps. Under a street lamp, they read the movie listings like death notices. All of people-less Fifth rang with Eli's implosion of disappointment. He was too upset to hit Carrie or even make a sound. He put on the face of a used car salesman – or it put him on: that heavy, generic American disappointment only men can know. They started uptown.

'What are we gonna do?' He finally whispered, wiped tears from his eyes.

'We can go tomorrow. We can go to a matinee.'

'Shut up with your fucking fifty-cent words. There are no *matinees* of *The Shining*, pus-head.'

'Let's get beers!' Arnie put an arm around each kid … and drank two pairs of Rolling Rocks on the way back uptown, so he was in a *great* mood, and wasn't really tripping at all anymore – thank god – by the time they got in to find Viv in the middle of changing the cat box.

It was a complicated business. The dirty litter was in a rectangle-mouthed Gristedes paper bag; the new litter was muckle-mouthed, torn at the top into a creepy grimace; the cat box was in the tub filled with hot water and Comet. Viv was bent over it, looking murderous with rubber gloves on. She was only wearing her purple leotard, and her short hair stuck straight up like Sid Vicious. Sweat dripped down from her forehead.

Eli ran in, 'I gotta piss so bad it's coming out my eyeballs, move!'

In the living room Viv, Arnie and Carrie regarded each other. Viv pulled her pants on and did up her belt wrong; the tail of an elephant was hooked to the tail of one further along. Eli came out of the bathroom without flushing and turned on the TV. Viv went back into the bathroom, flushed, and finished the litter. Carrie was standing in the center of the room, stock-still, watching *In Search Of* – a rerun about what the unborn child sees and can remember. It wasn't one of the scary ones – it wasn't about Bigfoot or the Loch Ness monster – but the music made it feel nerve-wracking, even as it showed a hypnotized woman remembering happy times in the womb. Moustachioed Leonard Nimoy asked her how it felt inside her mother when her mother laughed, and the woman smiled with her eyes closed and said, 'Good.'

'Know the psychic, Miss Rosa, over the smaller dry cleaners?' said Viv.

'What about her?'

'Uh huh.'

'Shhh! I'm trying to watch this. *Shit*.'

'I went for a reading. I *know*. Anyway *she* started telling *me* about *her* life. Very interesting. She is. That's the kind of person who really makes an impression.'

Arnie was smoking a Merit and leaning into the refrigerator, 'Why do people leave forks in plates of food. Why do people leave plates of food in the refrigerator with forks in them. I'll meet her. I want to know my future.'

Carrie said, 'Frozen dinners. That's your future, Arnie.' – without taking her eyes off the womb-woman, who was now sitting up in a chair talking to a psychiatrist.

The evening wound down.

Arnie put the contents of the freezer in the oven and then they all fought over the Celeste Individual Pepperoni Pizza, a Stouffer's Welsh Rarebit (no-one wanted that one) and a Lean Cuisine Boil-in-the-Bag Fettucini Alfredo.

Going to bed Eli did his 'gangsters versus cockroaches' routine for Carrie through the air vents at the top of the cheap plywood wall that divided the bedroom into their two rooms. She laughed and laughed and her body felt warm and itchy in her bed. After he shut up, as she lay there, she started to feel like she was being tipped and dropped. It was a familiar feeling, usually easy enough to induce. Her length moved fast, back and forth, up and down. She could tip at any angle. She was suspended.

At 2 a.m., Viv went into Eli's room and climbed up the ladder to his loftbed and looked at him sleeping. She climbed down and went into Carrie's room and looked at her, on her futon on the floor. Eli had been straight as a vampire. Carrie looked like she'd been flung across the bed.

At 3 a.m., Arnie stopped abruptly in the middle of sex because he kept imagining himself as a monkey, the one from the fucking Coco Puffs commercial. Fuckin Acid!

At 4 a.m., Carrie dreamed Nora was kidnapped and was going to be 'boiled in oil' unless a ransom was paid. The phrase stuck in her head. Her voice was low and croaky. 'There was something about a very long bow, and a porch swing, on the porch at Grandma and Grandpa's, and something about a ferry.' Viv scooted over so her daughter could lie down next to her. On the other side of Viv, pressed against the wall, Arnie didn't wake up, because this was all very quiet, and almost part of sleeping.

6. The Visceral

THE LUNCH LINE snakes around the clammy corners of the low-ceilinged cafeteria of William T. Sherman Elementary School. Carrie is waiting with Helena. The smell of grey string beans, canned peach bits and breaded fish is pissy, yet enticing. On the wall above the counter, where the large black ladies in white coats and hair nets stand, a sign in NY License Plate orange-and-black reads: MAX CAP: . It's blank. When they get up to the counter and Helena sees the fish up close, she calls it 'gooey', and walks away empty-handed.

They find two seats in the middle of a nine-foot, sweatsock grey marble-effect Formica-veneered plywood folding picnic table, on one of the little benches that are attached to it (so the whole thing it can be folded up and be put to the side of the hall, for gym). Carrie is number nine in a row of seated children. For a second – while they climb over, then squeeze themselves between the mass of other kids – Carrie remembers how in first grade she'd try to hear within the lunchroom roar all the sounds that made it up, each voice that composed its deafening drone; but it was only one sound – a cross between a loud buzz and the sound inside a shell… She'd made a buzzing herself, in her confusion; thinking it was everyone's job to add to it. But that was then. Now she had cool things to discuss with Helena.

Helena (cotton-candy pink, hi-water Naf Naf jumpsuit, red heart-shaped barrettes, raspberry lip gloss and a bored and exhausted expression – she did not sleep for the sound of her mother fucking) is standing beside Carrie and has laid out before them: two packs of Hubba Bubba bubblegum (raspberry and chocolate flavors); a Kit Kat; an Almond Joy;

and a spool of something flat and neon yellow. She examines the seals carefully.

'What if they like put cyanide in these?'

That very morning, Carrie had divulged to her largely ignorant constituency (she was Current Events Representative of class 513) that several people had died by taking poisoned Extra Strength Tylenol in Illinois. She had taken the clipping from her *attaché* and read it out. As she spoke her mouth got drier and drier, like the paper. But she was proud, and she went on without swallowing or going to the water fountain.

Carrie takes her tuna sandwich from the brown bag – aka dogshitbag – and unwraps it from its tinfoil while saying, 'Uh? – No! *Duh*! Fluke. One in a zillion. See this?'

'What? Can I like have half?' Helena flips her rich honey-colored hair.

'Yeah, but like see this? How the mayo' – Carrie tips the tinfoil up, vertically – 'flows in rivulets, down into little silver canyons?'

'God, *shut up.*' Helena takes a bite of the sandwich, then wraps a piece of the yellow tape around her index finger, and puts that in her mouth too.

'The FDA *approved* that stuff? *That's* what you should be worrying about.'

'I dunno. It's probably like *pending. Hair* is all T&A, tits and ass,' Helena says, with some difficulty, her finger still in her mouth.

She's picking up a more intriguing conversation, one they left off when Mrs Wellington told them to '*like* shut their mouths' during her lesson on pollution. Helena thought *Hair* was vulgar. Carrie felt it was a rollicking good time.

'No, it's not. It's good clean family fun. We tried to go to the midnight show of *The Shining* on my birthday after we didn't go yachting but it was sold out. *That's* not a family movie.' They had to speak very loudly, as if they were shouting – but with that strange, constrained cadence, that bell-like delivery of children's speech.

57

Helena presses one square of chocolate and one of raspberry Hubba Bubba into a compact brick on the table, and puts that into her mouth, too.

'For goodness' sake. Now you can't even close your mouth. '

'For *goodness' sake*?' That cracks Helena up. 'MMMI can. IS clozed,' Helena is laughing. Her stomach clenches to keep the tuna in her mouth, and – strangely – her nose, then she taps Carrie lightly on the top of her thistle head to say 'Ha ha!' Carrie says, 'This is 'cause Lawrence is at that funeral in Vermont. This would *not* occur if he was over there with his like brisket and ketchup on challah.'

Helena chokes and snarfs. Two great long threads of snot hang down from her nose, and dangle like her mother's best costume jewelry earrings. Her cheeks are puffed out, shiny, bright red. Her eyes tear and blue eyeliner clogs the corners and runs down her face to her neck.

Lunch ends with them convulsing on the floor of the cafeteria in total hysterics. A warden is called to stand them up. They both *almost* pee. They can't speak.

'You two stay here and do homework during recess. Enough is enough.'

This kills them. They feel like they are being punched. They are both singing the song *Enough is enough is enough I can't go on I can't go on* in their heads. It's one they both hate, and sing all the time. When they have calmed down a little Carrie says, 'Helena, lemme ask you something.'

'Yeah?'

'Do you think that the guy in *Hair*, when he dies – Berger – do you think that he *knows* he's gonna die? Do you think he is supposed to *know* at any point that he is going to die?'

'How the hell would I know.'

An hour later, after Phys. Ed. they had to take a quiz on 'Pollution'.

Carrie's Test:

1. D. correct answer, the greenhouse effect
2. A. correct answer, carbon
3. D. correct answer, resources
4. A. correct answer, solar power

Extra Credit: name and describe one way in which the chapters on pollution have helped you to think differently about our future.

Carrie's Extra Credit:

It May sound stange but the chaptars have made me think about the sun set. We learned that the reasun it is so gloryious on top of N.J is because of the pollution. I have been at my grandparents cuonty house in Rhinebeck (sp?) and the sun set their is plan orange. Here it has all the colors of the rainbowe melted together like a sorebay sunday. This has made me think it would be a sham, in some respects, for there to be no pollution. For the future I surpoise it would be worth it!

Helena was still working. Everyone was still working, breathing, ass-shifting. Radioactively-large grains of dust in streams of yellow sunlight landed on Carrie's old Current Events cut-outs pinned to the corkboard, on the green cursive alphabet stapled above it, and on Mrs Wellington's grey-copper dome of hair. There was only the soft sound of the points of No.2 pencils moving. Carrie liked this: the after-calm of a test you finish first.

* * *

Three days later on Thursday evening, Viv and Carrie are down in Riverside Park. These are the last of the warm days. Some days are warm, some are cold. In New York, the seasons have an almost perfect cycle. A storybook cycle. No weeks of fogs; no seasons of rain. In New York there are thunderstorms, baby cherry blossoms, arbors of roses, scorched grass, algae-covered lakes, mallard ducks returning, cold blue skies, windy nights, feet and feet of snow.

Viv was doing Tai Chi. She was on Cloud Hands, at the beginning of the third and final part of The Form. Lawrence Levy was down in the park, too. He had returned from sitting shivah in New England, and was standing, arms akimbo in the center of the track, daydreaming, not practicing his long-jump. Viv was under her favorite sycamore, moving like a windmill, or something with slow momentum, a ship's propeller. Carrie was sitting at Viv's feet, on a tree stump, moving her sneakers around in the track's gravel, wearing her spotless red Field Day uniform, all ready for Field Day tomorrow. She was also drawing a face on an old wooden peg. When she was finished, she put the peg in her *attaché* and vowed to carry it with her always. She thought, with the familiar mix of laxity and terror: if I lose this peg my mom will die. She ripped up some grass and shoved it in the case too. She had thought Viv would be done by now, but no. Carrie got up and rode her old bike back and forth from the disused baseball diamond on 69th to the rape tunnel at 83rd forty-nine times, then quit, because fifty seemed too complete. Lawrence was still in the centre of the track.

After staring at Carrie, and getting a response in the form of a shrug, Lawrence approached superciliously. 'Hello Mrs Martian. Hello Carrie.' And continued, 'You ready for the big' – he spread his arms towards the green in the center of the track – 'Field Day? We're gonna have a field day, Field Day, don't you think? You know you can't wait, Carrie.'

They went for a walk. They wandered up towards the baseball diamond and stopped at the edge of the underside of the West Side Highway, beside the off ramp that had not been finished: the elevated road just stopped there, dropped off like an open jaw. Something about Teamsters. Carrie looked out at hazy Faggot Dock, which had been used as lots of things.

'May I inquire, again, if you think you're gonna win the 400 meter?'

'Just shut up, Lawrence. Probably.'

'You don't think Marcy's gonna whip yer ass? Why do you carry that friggin' case everywhere? You're bonkers. They say that.'

Carrie said, 'Your shorts are *too* white.' He was all in white, being on the white team. His hair was too blonde. His side-part too neat. Even his crooked nose was too neatly crooked. He looked under the bridge, where it was dark.

'Wanna go under there?'

'Hell no in the middle of December when it's twenty below. You look too preppy. It's too much. You're trying too hard.'

It was very bright; the mist was bright. Lawrence shaded his eyes and stared at Carrie's knees under her red gym shorts. 'Is it true you drink a milkshake a day to keep from slipping down the drain?'

'Is it true you fuck Barbies in the shower?'

Lawrence paused, then bent and grabbed a clod of mud and flung it at Carrie's shirt. It was the look on his face though, not the mud. The you-get-what-you-deserve look. She walked stiffly back to Viv. Viv was almost finished with the last part of The Form. In the last five minutes the arms move in circles in opposite directions, and there's this tell-tale slo-mo karate chop.

When Viv saw Carrie she froze mid-chop and lowered her leg with an air of finality. 'What the *fuck* happened to Helena's shirt?' Carrie had borrowed it for Field Day because she didn't have a red shirt.

Carrie pointed at Lawrence, who had returned to stand in the long jump pit in the center of the field in the center of the track. His hands were back on his waist, his head cocked to one side. He was half a Jew. Helena used to say there was

61

one whole Jew in the room when Carrie and Lawrence were there. Carrie coached Lawrence on how to handle Helena – who was his girlfriend – when they went on dates. He should kiss her *at the end* of the date.

As angry Viv and sulky Carrie approached, Lawrence yelled and gestured from the shallow pit: 'But she started it Mrs Martian Cox! It's a friggin' double standard!'

She called to him, 'You'll *pay* for the dry cleaning bill.'

'Izod's hand wash only! It goes all stiff if you dry clean it!'

'What'd you say? What'd you say?'

'It's Helena's anyway!'

'You'll pay!'

'Ma!'

Forty-five seconds later, Carrie and Viv headed out of the park, only to be cut off by The Fat Crazy Guy, in his tweed greatcoat and Cat in the Hat scarf. He always wore the scarf wound once around his neck, and trailing along the ground. He stood ten feet from them, in the middle of the entrance to the rape tunnel, his hands in his coat pockets. Viv paused and put her hands on her waist. She stared him down.

'What's that you doin'? Kung Fuey?' He asked this twice a week.

Viv raised her eyebrows, said *Tai Chi*, and pulled Carrie along to the right of him, whispering so he could hear. 'Hold your breath, dear.'

He called after them, 'Stupid bitch', then shifted on his feet, dissatisfied.

Lawrence was watching from the sawdust in the center of the track, plotting revenge. But his fantasies kept resolving in him wiping tears off Carrie's face. '… and bitch in training!' The man in the greatcoat laughed, pleased with that line. It was the kind of thing they should put on a t-shirt and sell for eight bucks, he thought.

Viv and Carrie walked fast through the tunnel and out the other end where Viv stopped, turned around, and looked over the balustrade. The sun was setting behind the rectangular highrises of Jersey: copper, gold and LifeSavers-red, hot pink and lavender. At the very edge, where the light met the buildings, there was an outline of neon green.

'See, now, if we had Nora … Men are afraid of dogs.'

'I thought you said he read German. I wonder what his story is?'

'Well, he does – yes, he reads German.' They approached the crosswalk at Riverside Drive. Viv never crossed against the light. She always held Carrie's hand. She always looked both ways.

She looked both ways twice and tugged her. 'I think he's probably from a very good family, probably very well educated, but he's just schizophrenic. It runs in families – there's not one in ours, don't worry!' That faraway look in her eye again. The event had gone from actual to recountable. Viv could tell of freak accidents, birth defects, dyslexia, and somehow make it all seem … warranted, explicable, conspiratorial. A story. And once it's a story, you're in the clear.

Minutes later, at the West End Superette, Miss Rosa was buying a bottle of Manhattan Special Coffee Soda. Viv and Carrie had in their arms: a can of Mighty Dog, an Orangina, two Fosters oilcans, a square of Philly and a loaf of Branola. Viv was explaining to Carrie: 'I think Arnie has another girlfriend.'

Phoebe was checking out. She interrupted Viv and said hello to Carrie, and added, 'Aren't you a pretty pair!'

How were they to answer that? They smiled, and looked down at the huge cubes and rolls of meat under the refrigerated glass deli counter.

Moments later, back home, the elevator was moving very slowly, and knocking into the walls of the shaft: scraping them, swaying and bouncing, left and right, up and down. Carrie lowered herself into the corner and felt the center of gravity of the box on a cable. Viv hit the red alarm. The walls of the elevator were textured: green paint with gold flecks. It was hot. There was a vent on the ceiling. If you pried up the brass plate with concentric circles in the center of the floor, there was a vent there too. Sometimes Eli put his legs up on the polished brass handrails and made the elevator shake; but not *this* way. There was a little window you could watch the floors pass through. They were now stuck between floors and bouncing gravely.

'I don't think he has another girlfriend.'

'Oh he *does*.'

Enrique the New Super came with a crowbar – 'Hang on ladies!' – and they had to step up two feet to climb out onto the cool little tiles of the seventh floor landing. They took the stairs the rest of the way in silence. The stairwell windows were open wide, and let in the cool early-evening air with its smell of cooking onions and sounds of televisions in the courtyard. It had been 36 hours since Arnie had been home.

Carrie went to her bedroom, closed the plywood door, re-moved the cat screen (Viv was obsessive about keeping them in the windows at all times, because her first cat Kooky had fallen out the window and died) and leaned out. Phil Silver, the cameraman, was typing across the courtyard. He was next to a tall pile of paper. He had his glasses and no shirt on. She could only see above the line of the desk. He usually didn't have any underwear on either, though. Unlike the elderly couple down on 10. They had the TV and no other lights on. In the blue glow, his white bucket underpants milled around alone, as if possessed, while her torpedo bra floated above the couch.

Carrie turned into her slit of a room, and started packing her bag for the upcoming holiday weekend with her grand-parents. Stiff polyester pink 'traveling' pajamas; 'traveling' compact; 'grandparent trousers' that were Pretty Please brand and slightly too small, but not ripped. Pretty Please embossed on the right ass pocket. Viv suggested wearing her worst clothes, to get them to take her shopping, but that seemed evil. And she wanted to look good; to look the part, a well-off couple's grandchild. Her room was awful. She hated the yellow she had chosen at Ben Franklin Paints. Radiant Sunflower her ass! The *glare*! The bare bulb on the ceiling showed everything: all the cat hairs Viv shellacked to the floor with Mop'n'Glo. Fuck Lawrence! What *was* all this stuff? Thumbtacks, cassettes, Enquirers and TV Guides; cap-less markers, unused diaries locked shut, the keys missing; dirty stuffed animals that had been mock-tortured by Eli (haircuts, eye-removal, stitches, amputations, sex-change operations...) She wanted to be someone else.

She was going to her father's tomorrow night for Marilyn's show in Hoboken. He was picking them up from Field Day. Then she'd go on to her grandparents' house in Rhinebeck for Saturday Sunday and Monday (Columbus Day Holiday). Endless. None of those things had any appeal. She tried to think of something in the near future to look forward to. A trip to McDonald's would do. She racked her little brain as she packed her little pack, and then she stood up on her remaining shelf, and tried to hammer a sheet into the corners of her window, which worked. She was thinking about how to reaffix a lock to her door – about the tenth that Eli had simply pushed in – when Viv sauntered in, halfway through her first oilcan, looking at her manicure, and seeming to talk to herself. 'Give me Helena's Izod, sweetheart. I can just brush the mud off. That wasn't very good of old Lawrence, was it?' She looked up at the whack of the hammer. 'Why are you nailing that sheet to the window?'

'I need curtains. I have no privacy.'

Viv shrugged, took a deep breath and did a neck roll. 'That'll ruin it. That's my grandmother's linen sheet. That's an *heirloom*.' In the corner of the sheet there was a small rip where the nail was, like the eye of a ghost. THE HALLOWEEN PARADE! That's what there was to look forward to!

'I don't see what there is to *smile* about.' Viv considered taking the sheet down, but decided not to; anyway, it was against policy to contradict Carrie. She left Carrie there, three feet above her. Leaning on the window, dreaming up her Halloween costume.

Two hours later Viv had drank both the oilcans and eaten all the cream cheese on two slices of Branola (with a slice of Videlia onion) and was asleep in her clothes on the mustard couch which she hadn't bothered to unfold and make into a bed.

Carrie was also asleep, in her room, dreaming about a ghost in a sheet that was a kid dressed up as a ghost that was claiming it was *really* a ghost. Carrie was skeptical and not very scared in the dream. She was having a conversation with the ghost, on a suburban sidewalk she had never seen.

Arnie was asleep too, but he was on the 96th Street crosstown bus, on the way back to Viv's after two days with Lucy. He was so happy. He was in love. He was smiling in his sleep.

(I think Eli was at his friend Dylan's, but it might have been Eddie's. Viv and Carrie would have known, but it was so long ago I forget.)

7. Arnie Woods and the Berlin Work Needle

ARNIE HAD FORGOTTEN he was there. He was rolling and unrolling a five dollar bill, looking at himself in the mirror above the mantle in Miss Rosa's ex-ballroom. Then he remembered. He put the bill back in his front pocket and his arms at his sides and cleared this throat. Phoebe sat at the table, staring at her crystal ball, very erect. Arnie studied the mantle's center-piece – a Moreno glass clown . He picked the statue up – and examined the dust-coated folds of its multicolored greatcoat. He put it back with what he hoped was a disturbing *clunk*. Miss Rosa continued to stare at the ball. Arnie cleared his throat again and finished his cigarette and watched a plastic bag blow past the window. Eventually he went back to looking at himself in the mirror, and forgot where he was. Then she spoke. 'Don't you work at Gristedes?'

In one step he was in the chair opposite her, his legs spread wide and confident, trouser-creases pointing to the ceiling. 'Listen, this is like stupid, but I met this girl and we fucked, sorry, made love, for two days – and what I want to know is, I want to know if she's gonna call. Can't believe it but she's, I don't know. I just felt like I *knew* her.'

So *this* was the boy who knocked Viv up: he was the only white guy working at Greedy Brothers at the moment. Phoebe stared at a scar on his chin, a sickle shape, the size of a nickel. It was identical to a scar she had on her own chin; she touched her own. Coincidences. Hers was a kitchen 'accident'. Her mother had been holding her still, on her lap, with one hand, and peeling an acorn squash with the other. Phoebe was fourteen at the time. 'She loves you already. I'll give you that free. You can go.'

Arnie bounded up and was half way out the door, then froze. 'No. No that's not right.' He took the rolled up five from his pocket and put it in front of her on the tablecloth.

She held it to her nostril. 'You shouldn't snort so much cocaine.'

'That's not for coke – Jeez. Just a nervous habit. I roll things. Like all the time. Like give me like *a frying pan,* and I'll try to roll it.' He took back the five, unrolled it, and carefully licked the edges at an angle so he wouldn't get a paper cut on his tongue.

'You know Viv?'

The coke made Arnie's lips pucker. They seemed to get stuck in the pucker as Miss Rosa continued. 'I can help you out of that mess with the least collateral damage if you do me a favor: come over from time to time and listen to me. I have some things I need to say. I have to tell someone some things.'

'That *blackmail*? Christ, you're small stakes, lady! Ha! OK talk to me. ' He looked at his Casio: twenty nine minutes till his shift under Gristedes, repacking meat, putting new red stuff on top of the grey.

On the day she was returned from the Apthorp as faulty, her father Cotton had an accident. She was staring down at the dirt field, ignoring the storm moving in, dreading her future, avoiding her Berlin Work, when there was a loud, clogged screech, like a swan's hiss. She jumped up, or tried to – she fell comically, her legs sliding under her – then re-membered to untie the bow from the swing. She ran into the darkening house.

'Wait. Who? What? Where? Like *when*?' Arnie ejaculated.

'You sound stupider than you look. Just listen.'

She followed the noise and found him in the kitchen, rolling on the floor, spreading a pancake-sized smear of blood. He was wearing his usual: overalls, his little cap – it had fallen to the side; the type of cap meant he was gay, to anyone who knew the local signs – and only one workboot. There was thunder now and it was pouring. Cotton pulled himself up on her, climbing her – lightning struck – and she saw his expression: he seemed to be trying to suck his mouth, nose and eyes back into his face. She felt his heart through his shirt and smelled him. He smelled like he always did, like cut wood that had sat in the damp overnight. Then he crumbled to the floor again and slithered. She wanted to ask what was wrong – she liked her father more than Lucretia – but that seemed idiotic. Surely it must be obvious. She was frozen. All she could see were the new white candlesticks framed in the grey kitchen window. She felt like a candlestick. Stiff and wax, like a character in some weird tale.

She followed as he crawled down the hall on Lucretia's prized Berlin Work runner. Six months of needling: a series of cloistered unicorns, in black squares with white polka dots around the edges, like a reel of film. Cotton kept reaching up, punching the walls and pulling down other stitched scenes, framed ones. Phoebe stepped on and cracked the glass of her mother's favorite: a city lady, her arms swallowed in an enormous muff. There was more thunder.

From upstairs Lucretia groaned from her bed, 'Cot-'un? Phoebe?'

When they got to the drawing room – which was lit up dim and orange by a streetlamp – he tore the top two drawers from a bowed cupboard and threw them across the room. They hit and left a deep scratch in the wainscoting. He kneaded the drawers: itsy bits of lace, cut-outs from the Ladies Home Journal, a daguerreotype of Aunt Hilda she'd sent around as a Christmas card – it skidded to Phoebe's feet and stared orangely up at her: Hilda was dressed as Abraham Lincoln, and her black half-brother Cyrus (also Cotton's half brother, of course, but that was never mentioned) was playing John Wilkes Booth. Cotton grabbed at his daughter's dress and pulled her down next to him. She kicked him in the chest with both feet, like a clockwork toy. Nothing she was doing made any sense to her. Despite the rough kicks he was taking, her father held fast and slashed a strip of her hem.

And only then did she see his left heel. A Berlin Work needle, the largest – the one used for shrubbery and skies – stuck half out of it, and had left a two-inch, gaping red slit where it had pulled.

'Cot-'un?' came the falsetto Lucretia reserved for very special occasions.

Her father lifted his chin and looked at Phoebe. She pulled the needle – a circle of flesh came up as she yanked it out, like a tiny plunger. Then she tied the strip of hem around his foot. Phoebe and her father looked at each other. She leaned back on her elbow and rested her head in her palm, her neck against the wood claw of the settee. They watched his blood soak through her hem. In the room there was … there was something new between them: a clear, calm understanding.

Phoebe tried to quickly glance at Arnie. She didn't want to look like she was worried she was boring him. It came out as a sort of shudder.

While they were still on the floor, the knocker hit the front door three times. Phoebe smoothed her greasy hair, helped Cotton up, and went to get it.

Aunt Hilda stood in the frame. The giant, yellow post-storm sun sat on the tip of the church steeple behind her.

'Spot of trouble?' Hilda said.

Cotton was dragging his way up the banister to the landing. He called down. 'Hilda.' He used women's names to mean everything: *pass the butter; the butter's rancid; shush; come here; I love you.*

When he was out of earshot Phoebe whispered. 'Dad got a Berlin needle stuck up his foot.'

Hilda giggled and Phoebe accepted her white wool coat and held it over her own mouth. The coat smelled of orange blossom water. They were both staring at a stitched scene that lay intact on the floor, of couples ice-skating arm and arm on a frozen pond. Without looking up Hilda said, 'What happened to the Apthorp?'

'I'm not fucking psychic.'

They *really* laughed now, too loud. Then looked up, because the stairs creaked with the weight of Cotton and his wife. He carried her in one arm, her thighs and torso tucked up together like a bucket. They swayed slightly.

Phoebe and Hilda bit the insides of their mouths.

'Phoebe, *do* switch on the light bulbs and hang your Aunt's coat!' Lucretia called sternly, as if there was nothing unusual about her position. And indeed there wasn't. She always lost feeling in her legs around three in the afternoon. It came back the next morning.

Arnie opened his eyes: he'd been silent with his hands on the table, fingertips touching fingertips, half-listening. 'That was great. A real eye-opener. I gotta go. I gotta reshape the hamburger. I'll come back.' Then he reached out and patted the old lady on her head.

When he was gone Phoebe put her head on the table and wept.

8. After Field Day, Before Amsterdam is Broadway

AFTER FIELD DAY, Eli held his head in his hands as he and Carrie waited at the track for their dad to pick them up. They sat in the concrete bleachers, opposite the track – its tan grass, its row of cherry trees full of drab green autumn leaves – and the Hudson, which was white-tipped and moving fast. The kids had their book bags, weekend-stuffed, at their feet. They brought: 'punk' clothes for the photo show Ethan was taking them to tonight in Hoboken; 'presentable' clothes for their grandparents house on Saturday, Sunday and Monday; toothbrushes; Pepsodent; horror novels; Eli's Sony Walkman; Carrie's modified stuffed animals.

As they waited, they discussed their own, their friends' and their enemies' victories and defeats. Eli went on a long riff about Carrie's asinine entry into the Funny Hat Contest. She'd tied a stuffed dog to a frisbee with a scarf as she was running out the door. Raising his face for the first time, he stuck it on her head and fixed the scarf under her chin. Eli's first-prize-winning, blue-ribbon, very funny 'hat' – a demon washing machine he called Frankie – sat beside them, dwarfing them. Eli'd got the guys at Radio Shack to save him a 'bonafide' Maytag Washing Machine cardboard box. Its 'possessed' face glowered, oddly peaceful in its huge stillness: a smeared line of a mouth (Viv's coral lipstick), paper-plate eyes with lightning bloodshot lines and real blonde hair (Carrie's clippings) glued on to make big bushy eyebrows, a 'skin-colored' face (Eli had mottled the box with a damp sponge dipped in white pancake). He was so proud of it that his own face was bothering him. It felt like someone else's;

that's why he was holding it. The sun sank a little lower over the highrises. After-work joggers appeared on the track. The only evidence of The William T Sherman School Field Day were the empty bags of chips and Twinkie wrappers blowing around. Eli watched through threaded fingers.

When they had covered each sporting event – the relays, the dashes, the long-jumps – Eli and Carrie went back over them again in minute detail, the kind of talk that always leads to bickering. Pink clouds shaped like dashes moved along the sharp edge of Jersey's Palisades. They'd reached a blank in the conversation. There must have been more to the day! They were desperate, each in their own way, to keep talking, otherwise they would have to face the fact that nothing was happening. Things were not going according to plan. Carrie watched a Cesna trailing a banner as it flew above the center of the river. *Donna will you still marry me?* Ethan was forty-five minutes late. Half an hour happens; 45 minutes, and something's up – or *not* up, more like – fast asleep.

'Why you like Speedy Gonzalez? You eat Wheaties an' shit in the closet? Your legs are like a cricket.' Eli stood and began *bothering* Carrie about her victories. She'd won the 400 meter, the 800 meter, and saved the red team's relay race. '*Annnnnnddddd* you're a fucking bleedin' heart liberal.' He was referring to when Carrie went over to console Lida, who Carrie had beaten in every race she won. 'Serves you right she threw you on your ass.' Lida had pushed Carrie onto her ass and muttered, 'Stupid white bitch.'

Carrie stared ahead, caring only very mildly about Lida – mainly over the ethical issues it raised (was winning inherently bad?) – but really not giving a flying fuck what Eli had to say about it. Eli was bothering *himself* again by mistake. Realizing this, he shut up and looked all around. Sun almost down. He put Frankie on his head; it was the only way he could carry it. His muffled voice came through the box. 'You gotta wait here. Tell him I'm at Dylan's if he shows.'

73

It had been a nice bright day, but it was getting cold. A lady came up to Carrie. She smelled of baby powder; she had short black hair and a permanent; she wore pink terry shorts with pantyhose under them and squinted down at Carrie as if Carrie's face were emitting light. 'Are you OK? Are you all alone?'

'Yeah, I'm just waiting for someone. Someone's meeting me.' Carrie smiled reassuringly then watched her as she started her extremely slow jog around the track. Carrie thought the lady should do something with her hands at the same time. Like knit. It was *so* slow it was like she was underwater. What a waste of time! All the fucking waiting! Meanwhile, a very thorough Puerto Rican picnic with disposable barbecue was getting set up in the middle of the track. A fat old matriarch, surrounded by younger men with moustaches and sunglasses, and circling toddlers, stared at Carrie, who had forgotten she still had the frisbee-dog-hat on. The fat lady took her hands off her hula-hoop waist and went back to her preparations. Carrie decided she would wait until the hot dogs were cooked.

When they started eating, Carrie rose, put Eli's backpack on her front, her own on her back, and went home.

The door was unlocked, as usual. Nora, sweet and excited to see her, ran over and pissed and shat on a piece of the *Times* that was spread on top of a Gristedes bag for that purpose. *There Goes Rhymin' Simon* was still on the record player. It was turning, the needle knocking the smooth end of the black then jumping back, again and again. Carrie lifted it to 'Was a Sunny Day'. Then she took the dog shit out on the paper, and threw it down the garbage chute in the back hall.

Twenty minutes later Arnie came in. She was spotlit in the final reflected red sunbeam, the phone receiver on her ear, standing over a stack of folded clothes with cat puke on it, wondering whether it still counted as 'clean laundry' because all there was to do to restore it was to pull little bits

74

of half-digested Nine Lives from a couple of cuffs with a kitchen scrubber sponge. She'd called her father's loft eight times; this was the ninth. She'd let the phone ring twenty times, which was her standard number. She hung up and explained to Arnie why she was there, but he didn't realize she wasn't supposed to be, which took the frisson out of it.

'This place is a wreck,' he said.

'I know. Everytime you turn around there's another pile of like unidentifiable shit.'

'First get everything up off the floor.' Arnie shook his fist emphatically, a cigarette poking out from between his fingers. 'Then, and only then – surfaces.'

He walked back to the darkening living room and jumped onto the couch à la the Fonz, throwing his Fayvas up.

Carrie stayed at the kitchen sill, staring at the McDonald's building on Amsterdam. She was thinking: It's Friday evening. Since her dad had not arrived at Field Day, as planned, to take them to the rescheduled photo show tonight and to Rhinebeck tomorrow, future plans remained utterly unclear. It wasn't actually Amsterdam Avenue, out the window, she was also thinking. It was An Unknown Address, right there, the McDonald's Building, where Amsterdam Avenue *turns into* Broadway, but where it isn't called Broadway yet. The avenues like reins, or a skipping rope, lifted gently, and then allowed to land, crossed. The McDonald's building's designation was confusing to residents, to *postmen* even. Isn't it a shame that there is no order where there should be, but lots and lots where it can never *truly exist?* Carrie tried to remember what she was looking forward to. She re-cataloged her list and could only come up with annoyingly long-term goals. Leather briefcase; Doctor of people, or of something; a beach house. She'd *forgotten* the Halloween Parade. She was like that. She thought so hard she forgot things.

She heard noises in the attic above the guest bedroom on Pumpkin Lane, near Rhinebeck, where she could only assume they were still going tonight. Or *should* she assume it? Should she call her grandparents, who were already in their country house expecting them? She remained at the window, and gave into dreading their house. The bed she slept in – in 'Grandma Esther's Room' – was harder than the slanted wooden floor. On the bookshelves there were Ladies' Home Journals. Miles of Ladies' Home Journals, spanning her grandfather's tenure as Editor-in-Chief. In the center of the room, on an old dresser between the windows choked of light by the 20-foot tall Leylandii hedge, beside the weird antique lamp with its globular ochre glass lampshade (one of a lost pair), sat an old Little Black Sambo doll. He was one of the antiques that came with the house. His white eyes glowed at Carrie through the night.

But these artifacts – the lamp and Sambo, Grandma Esther's deathbed and the acres of feminist magazines – had nothing on the old well. *Yes*, it was ancient. *Yes*, the house was over two hundred years old, and the birthplace of a lesbian arts colony gone fractious, or something. She understood the need; she understood 'preserving heritage'. Thus Sambo and his downstairs brother, the dented Blackamoor, weren't rascist: they were among liberals, so they were 'American Folk Art'. She got all that. But something about *the fucking old pump*, its thick, rusted handle like a swan's neck. Its situation in an indent *and* a swell in the front lawn, as if the swell had grown up around it, like a pimple. Carrie had to turn her face as far in the other direction, up toward the falling-apart wooden shack on the hill (as she thought about it, she unconsciously turned from the window and stared at the back door of the kitchen) to avoid the well's murky little sneer. As if it *knew* things. She'd never had such distaste for a thing before. She'd always felt an intense, simple pity for the inanimate, but this disgust and fear was the first of many object-aversions. They aren't all innocents.

The day she'd realized the extent of her hatred of it, her grandfather was taking some head-shots of her and Eli.

They were posing at the well. Viv had had the brilliant idea that they should 'break into commercials.' In between rolls of film, they played with it, because Grandpa said if they pumped and pumped and pumped ... and it did. It put forth one drop of grey water. That was the worst.

(Carrie was now trying to stuff some of the clothes she'd removed the cat puke from into the dresser in the hall. The drawer had to be opened from a very specific and awkward angle, as it was bust. The pile was falling out of her arm, and she was looking up at a Berlin Work piece, a fruit bowl, by some dead old lady relative.) The weekend before last she had put on her two best mismatched earrings, hairspray, a Polo sweater Helena had loaned her – and was all ready for the photo show. But it was cancelled because the photographer, Marilyn, had OD'd. Supposedly it was rescheduled for today. But now Ethan had not shown up.

The weekend before last, she and Eli had spent an hour in the mirror doing their hair, putting on eyeliner. They were to be picked up by the chauffeured limo, then on to a fancy Italian restaurant – The San Remo – and finally driven under the river to the show in Hoboken. This week Carrie had not stopped wondering if she should go to the trouble again. It wasn't about the effort. Effort Schmeffort. It was just – how could her heart be in it, if the first time was a dress rehearsal, a fake? She couldn't feel the same excitement again. Ethan had been *tres* agitated when he arrived, overwhelmed with guilt, because Eli had been talking about the limo for two fucking months. So Ethan had drugged himself sentimental and rented a limo on his Diners Club card – *anyway*. All they did was ride it downtown and get out in front of a Moroc-can restaurant that Ethan said was known for its marinated meats. He didn't order any kebabs, however; he drank three frozen banana daiquiris, then puked them back up at the loft while the kids watched *Godzilla vs. Mothra* on Channel 11.

Such was no-time. Faked time. Here Carrie stood: afraid of Rhinebeck, of the well; unable to close the dresser drawer because she had over-filled it *and* it hated her; eleven years old since only one week ago; and wondering what might happen next. Or what was supposed to have already happened. Or if *anything* ever happened the way it was supposed to.

The phone rang and Arnie got it. 'It's for you. *Is a boy.*'

Carrie went into the dull kitchen. The sunset was over. 'Yeah?'

'I wanted to apologize, Carrie. I'm sorry I threw mud at you. I thought you performed exceptionally this afternoon, and I thought Lida was very ungracious.'

'Shut up Lawrence. What do you really want?'

'I wanted to say I was sorry.'

'I forgive you.'

'Good. Helena and I are going for a slice in an hour. What should I order?'

'Nothing wimpy. Sicilian.'

'I hate Sicilian. It's like eating a stuffed animal. I want anchovies.'

'Not a good idea.'

'Can't you meet us? We can pretend it was just a coincidence.'

'There are no coincidences. I wouldn't be going for a slice by myself. Where?'

'The fucking pizza place on her block, Pizza Joint. Where do you fucking think?'

'I'm busy.'

'Come on, please Carrie. See – you're still mad about the mud. I'm very sensitive about my appearance. You know how upset I was not to get the part in Silver Spoons. I could have *been* somebody. But no, no: they wanted Ricky Schroeder. Ricky Schroeder! He's forty years old.' Lawrence was an actor. He had head shots and everything. They even said *Lawrence Leslie* along the bottom of the glossy 8x10's because Levy sounded too Jewish.

'OK. OK. OK. I might happen by.' She hung up.

Arnie had Nora on the leash. 'Come to the park with us?' he said. Carrie felt sorry for him because the call wasn't Lucy.

She wasn't sure. She thought maybe she should stay in case her dad or the Martians or Eli called.

Arnie said, 'I'll clean the house when we get back. Please.'

'OK. OK. OK.'

9. The Boat Basin

'OK?'

'OK.' She didn't really want him to, but he insisted.

'OK!' Arnie zipped up Carrie's jacket, the down 'blue snot' she hated.

When they were by the river they stood in front of the boat basin, in the drizzle, admiring the yachts, choosing the ones they'd have. Arnie liked a pointed number called *The Monsoon*. Brown water lapped at it. They boats were behind a fifteen-foot barbed wire fence. Steam came off the Hudson, even though it was cold and raining lightly. Carrie saw some pieces of shit floating around, glistening in the lamplight. Carrie liked a square houseboat that was berthed too far in to see the name, but I remember it was called *Meander*. It had a terrace and trellises and two white wicker chairs with brown cushions. Carrie said: Mom always said it'd be a nightmare to live on a boat: rats. Arnie said: your ma thinks she knows everything.

Carrie said, 'She does know everything. She knows all and sees all.'

'Did you at least win yer race at Field Day, wierdo?'

'Yeah, who cares.'

'D'ya get a medal?'

She took three gold-painted bits of plastic on red, white and blue ribbons out of her tight jeans' pocket and gave them to him. An old man dragging a beagle made his way up the dock and opened the gate; Arnie caught it before it shut, walked through it and held his hand back to Carrie.

'Don't be chickenshit.'

'We'll get arrested. It's breaking and entering.'

'It's *entering*.'

Under his feet the floating sidewalk bounced. It was starting to rain harder. She went in. Arnie pulled her blue snot hood up. Coming off the main walkway were littler, floaty walkways, marked with letters. They walked to Z and looked across the river. New Jersey looked friendly as a Christmas tree, the headlights in a line along the road at the edge of the river, moving and glowing, orange and sparkling blue.

'There is like *no one here*. Let's *break* into one.'

'Hell no.'

'Chicken.'

'God, Fine! That one. The house. The owners live in Florida.'

'No. Monsoon! Monsoon!' He held onto a non-existent hat and pretended to be blown along towards it.

The lights were on inside, but they were always on, as a *deterrent*. They pressed their faces near the window and saw a glass table with fake yellow roses on it. A sideboard with booze in decanters, with little necklaces with their names on them. A white-and-gold plastic princess phone on an end table. Two large palm plants on either side of a small sofa. It looked like a set.

'They're *never* here.' He stepped onto the deck with a wide step. Up and down the level of the park went.

Carrie stayed on the dock. Arnie went in. He poured out a 'Whiskey' and sat down at the table. Carrie watched him through the window. It was pouring. In the river she saw a weirdly-shaped garbage bag stuck to the bottom of a boat. Some boys were very far away, heading into the rape tunnel. Carrie decided to go in too. Arnie was on the phone saying, 'That'll be the day.' Then he laughed and said 'Numchucks of course,' then 'I gotta go,' and hung up. He stubbed out the end of his Merit and exhaled through his words, 'Come to think of it, I'm not gonna smoke in here. They might not like it. And though I'm a thief and a fool I have no sense of decency.'

'Don't you mean you *do*? And don't you mean *sense of respect*? I can't believe you're cheating on my ma.'

Arnie put his drink down decisively and gave Carrie a long look. Then he said, 'Viv thinks love is a crock of shit. Those are *her* words. You think that? That your boyfriend on the phone back there?'

'No.'

Arnie looked at his hand around the crystal glass, 'Any idea why these are called snifters?'

'No. Let's go.'

A few years ago Ethan drew a pot-doodle and stuck it on his wall. It was a big boat almost as tall as it was long, a tugboat, maybe. It had the title written in underneath: *Carrie and Eli in Naive Boat*. NAVE she thought it was, and BOOT, because she could not read too well at that time, and it looked like one, a boot; it had smokestacks on the deck that looked like an ankle. When Eli told her it said naïve, she said she could not see how she was naïve: what didn't she know? What *exactly* didn't she know?

'You should see this girl, Carrie!'

Carrie was squished next to Arnie on the couch. He put his hand over her knee and his arm around her and gave her waist a hug. 'What soap do you use?'

'Dial, I think.'

'What am I meant to do? I mean I'm too young for Viv. I'm closer to *your* age than I am to hers. *You* should call me when you're 19. Lucy, this girl I met. Remember, when we were on line for *The Shining*, that gorgeous girl I was talking to?'

'You said you knew her from High School.'

'Well I *thought* I knew her from somewhere, but *apparently* I didn't. Anyway, Carr, you gotta meet her! She's a black belt in Wing Chung Kung Fu. She looks like Irene Cara. She has green eyes but she's black. She's an actress. And dancer.'

'I think you should tell my ma and she'll throw you out.'

'Yeah, I know, I'm gonna.' Carrie put her face in the arm-pit of Arnie's corduroy jacket then moved it up to his neck.

He was always warm but never sweaty. She liked his smell, cigarettes and Dr. Pepper; she liked the feel of his smooth face right after he shaved; it had resistance. She loved these things. She loved when he came in and slept in her twin bed when he had had a million Rolling Rocks. He held her very close and tight, like he did now. Someone knocked at the window of the boat. The dog walker. They stayed still for a moment, looking at each other, whispering about what the fuck to do.

'What should we do?'

'What *the fuck* should we do?'

'*I* don't fucking know.'

Arnie got to the door in one step. 'Yes?'

The man had his hood up and said, 'Who are you?'

'Mackenzie's nephew, this is my sis. We shouldn't have stopped by. I mean I knew they weren't here, but she was like really upset. She lost all her races at Field Day.'

'Jill and Fred don't have any children, or nephews. Who the hell *are* you?' He jerked his inert beagle's thick leather leash.

Arnie ran his hands through his hair and frowned. Carrie picked Nora up and said, very politely, 'I think she has to go. Excuse me sir. I'll just wait out here.'

She closed the door behind her and walked fast. The gate to the Boat Basin had a red button that said exit. She pushed, it clicked, and she was free. She daren't look back. She hoped he wouldn't get arrested.

She didn't want to go home. She didn't want to have to tell Viv where she had been. She decided to 'run into' Lawrence and Helena at the Pizza Joint after all. Carrie rushed. Nora pulled backwards, at her usual angle; she always seemed to want to get somewhere in the region of Atlantic City. Carrie spoke to her, 'Come on ya crazy mutt, you gonna roll Big Money, Big Money!' Leaving the park, she saw the two boys she'd seen earlier from the boat basin, racing around and around the basketball courts, soaking wet, hoods up, their hands cupped down in what they thought was an aerodynamic shape. The highway beside the court was gridlocked heading uptown. Steam was coming off the still cars.

When she got to Broadway, Carrie saw Lawrence from way the fuck across the street. He had his green snot on, with the hood up. He was outside Pizza Joint, under its dripping awning.

'You're loitering. Where's Helena?'

'I tried to kiss her and she got pissed off. You wanna slice? *Sicilian*?'

Carrie's face, jeans and dog were soaking wet. 'That was like so stupid! You know not to kiss her first! Have I like taught you *nothing*…' The pizza smelled great. 'I don't have money for pizza. Jesus.'

'Nevermind. Helena would get mad if I spent the buck I saved for her on you. I'll walk you home.'

Lawrence took hold of Nora's leash and pushed Carrie to walk on the inside, near the buildings, while he went by the road. He said, 'I don't want to be a cad. Ladies by the buildings, so they don't get splashed.' He'd been watching Robert Redford in *The Great Gatsby* on Betamax all month.

'Why would you kiss her *before* dinner? Why? That's a *cad*, you retard.'

'Spontaneity, Carrie.' Lawrence did a 'no one gets me' headshake, with added non-existent-beard scratch. The fucking head shake. She shoved him over to the building side, tripping over Nora, who yelped. Carrie and Lawrence struggled. Lawrence was saying – dragging her back towards the doormen buildings – 'I will *not* be a cad. I won't.' He won.

'Fine, fuckface.' Carrie was sweating under the blue snot, and her face was pink.

Carrie was tired and hungry and, finally, confused. Lawrence confused her. He was always being ironic. *Always*. In front of the doorman he said, 'Goodnight, dear,' smirked, kissed her cheek, and walked away.

This upset her excessively. She was starving. She screamed after him, 'You're a total dipshit!' The doorman gave her a look. She didn't think of the word dipshit as being a curse, but now that she saw Jose's face she realized: it *did* have the word 'shit' in it.

(Arnie didn't get arrested. But he did have to suck the old man's dick so he wouldn't call the cops. Arnie could tell he would have to, too, from the instant he opened the door of *The Monsoon*. Arnie could see that the man thought he was scum, because of Carrie. Ha. It was funny, he'd reflected later, on the way home – it had stopped raining and he could see stars above Central Park – it was funny: Lucy, in one fell swoop, had made certain sex acts unbearable. He now only wanted to suck on things that were lovely and sweet. He had no room in his head for cruel scenarios. They'd evaporated. They left this smooth young girl like a flat coke, sweet and warm, with no edge. He'd gone over to her house on the crosstown bus. She only had a half hour. He said, 'I know you love me; a two-bit psychic told me.' She didn't say anything. They fucked standing up in the kitchen, Arnie looking out the window and feeling a weight lifted from every cubic inch of his body. Someone so perfect. Someone he didn't even know he'd needed. He came back West, through Central Park, on foot. Saw the stars. It was nine. Walking through The Ramble in the dark, half a dozen guys approached him wanting to return the favour. But like I said, he was in love, not in the mood.)

10. Vanity Kills

'MOM, I'M NOT in the fucking mood.'

Rhinebeck was cancelled, but as it turned out the Martians were still in town, so Carrie was obliged to have a late dinner at their five-bedroom apartment on 1st Avenue. The Blue Snot was sodden but Viv said she had better go get on the bus right away. There was no time to change, and besides she didn't have another one.

'I hate that bus. I could crawl faster. Why isn't Eli coming? Those fucking game hens!...' They were the worst of Grandma Martian's recipes. Miniature chickens, weirdly sweet, encrusted in pulverized Cornflakes and dangerously undercooked.

Viv cut her off. 'Oh, she won't serve those *again*. Anyway Eli and Dylan went to *The Shining* – you know how he's dying to see it – they found a showing at the Museum of Modern Art, of all places. I'm a little hysterical. I need to appear together to the Martians, and neither my son nor husband can be located! So you need to go, now! Be a goodwill ambassador, sweetheart. Leave us not forget – the Martians pay our rent. God, where *is* Arnie? Any idea?' Viv was on something new. A new bag of pot. *Leave us not forget?* Plus Carrie really didn't want to talk about Arnie.

'OK. OK. OK.'

She ran into her room and grabbed her *attaché*, then took a deep breath, and left, running down the eleven flights of stairs and across the street to the bus shelter, where she waited half an hour; she watched the doorman read his Post through the steamed-up lobby window. She thought about her thoughts. When she was 8 and 9, she would will herself to forget *everything*, and then she felt that … rocking in her body. You had to close your eyes and make it come. A vibration rose into you. Your body felt like a hammock hung between trees rooted in clouds that went up and down and side to side; you looked normal but you were on a fast, bed swing. She could still do it, but now there was too much to figure out and arrange in the world … who had time to call up amniotic rocking?

There she was, in the bus shelter. As seen by passing cars: lit, and left invisible; lit, and left a blue blur. As seen by dog walkers, the dark circles under her eyes were almost the same color grey-blue as her irises. As seen by people looking out their windows down at the rainy street, she was a girl running her hands over the top of her white hair as if smoothing it; she was feeling for tiny bulges, which she pushed flat then felt rise up again.

All that time, standing still in the dark and feeling as still as she was, she kept fantasizing about her Red Devil Costume. She wanted thick French braids, the white equivalent of Lucy's cornrows. She wanted black fishnet tights and a long red sateen tail. She wanted a gauzy red cape. (Here you might imagine the sound of the windshield wipers on the bus, the passengers watching the wet buildings along 57th Street, the baroque facade of the brownstone Russian Tearoom, the closed shops with lit up signs and dark interiors: *Charavari, Bonwit Teller, Hammacher Schlemer* rolling past, the old ladies who got on, sat for an avenue or two, then alighted.) The girl she imagined looked nothing like her. Was a woman, actually.

The one thing she was meant to keep from her grandparents was that Arnie Woods lived with them – because then they would have contributed less towards the rent, *leave us not forget*. She was also not supposed to mention the drugs her parents took, but that wasn't likely to come up. Arnie, though…

Grandma Martian (in her home pronounced Mart-Ian, but nowhere else) – with her short puff-sleeved purple mohair sweater and antique plates and classy cheese dip, her hair cut in a stylish 'wedge' – said, 'Took you a while?'

'I almost got arrested! Arnie convinced me to go onto this houseboat and then we got *caught*.' Her grandmother took the Blue Snot, frowned at it, closed the coat-closet door and took it into the bathroom, where she hung it over the shower rail.

Her grandfather Martian had come into the living room from his study. He had an open book spread over his long fingers. 'Arnie?'

'Arnie, mom's boyfriend? He *lives* with us?' She said it though a mouthful of cheese and breadstick. The Martians always had things to tide you over laid out on a low Chinese papier-mâché table when you arrived. It was covered in Chinese logographs. There was a nest of them; little tables lived under the big ones. When she was very young she used to stack and unstack them.

Grandpa closed the book. *I and Thou*, Martin Buber.

'What's Arnie like?' He smiled at his wife, who rolled her eyes and went into the kitchen.

Carrie swallowed the breadstick with difficulty and started to sweat, 'Umgh, nice.'

They went to the dining room and sat down at a grey marble table, beside a floor-to-ceiling mirror. Carrie could not avoid looking at herself: hunched, slurping. She ate her curried carrot soup, had two bowls while answering questions – sweat beading on her forehead – about what books she'd been reading. *Cujo* and *Oliver Twist*. She removed them from her backgammon case and put them beside her on the table, staring at them as she spoke. Some dried pot leaves and grass fell out of the pages of the book and from the seams of the case. Carrie hadn't got more than ten pages into either book, and was annoyed at having to pretend she had. She'd seen *Oliver!* though. Her class had been taken uptown on the IRT, to Harlem, where they watched kids she could not believe were her age perform. They were absolutely incredible. Plus they were grown-ups: they had tits and beards. The show made Carrie and Helena *cry*.

She was very relieved when Grandma Martian interrupted her. Taking Carrie's bowl she went into the kitchen while settling into one of her usual exegeses; today, on what she called 'the kvetch novel' (she'd been reading Erica Jong): women writers, often Jewish like herself, who had had 'food and heat and a good education', complaining about their parents, their neighbors, their husbands, their sex lives.

'But' – Carrie watched as her grandmother took a tray of Cornish game hens out of the oven – 'Eli is such a fuck. Sorry. What I mean is – maybe there are times when even if you have food and aren't in a concentration camp you've got cause, or a right, to complain. I mean look at this bald patch.' Carrie lifted the flap of hair over her ear.

Grandpa Martian went red and stood up, 'We don't speak of concentration camps lightly, or use them as metaphors here. Or say *fuck.*'

Carrie looked down and did her best invisible weeping. She just meant … even if it wasn't *that bad*…

Florence, the retired social worker specializing in violent insane drug addicts, changed course. 'Oh, sit down. That's a subtle point to get up in arms about.'

'The holocaust was not subtle, Florence.'

She ignored him. 'All I mean, Carrie, is there are lots of people out there with a lot worse to contend with. I think these ladies should write about *someone* else. I'm not saying they don't have talent. They do! That's what I think. *A Tree Grows in Brooklyn* – try reading *that* Carrie. I mean, Murray, you like Erica Jong – but I get sick of her complaining, and honestly I don't want to *know* all the gory details. Make something up, for God's sake!'

'I know Erica quite well. A lovely woman, extremely bright. She doesn't *want* to make things up. She's … *pertinent*. She says things women weren't allowed to say twenty years ago.' He glanced at Carrie and shook his head, then went back to his delicate little hen.

Carrie's bird was already a macabre pile of tiny bones.

'Be that as it may. She should stop kvetching! She grew up in a nice doorman building.'

Murray chewed slowly, breathing deeply through his nose, then said with a labored air of commitment, like someone turning a car around, 'My father tried to push me in front of a milk truck in Brooklyn when I was nine. He dragged me to the curb and threw me in the road. He thought I was too soft … In those days, that was the worst thing a man could be, soft. Girly. I tried to teach Ethan the opposite. We have to watch *any* generalizations, Carrie. Remember that. In those days the worst thing a man could be was like a woman. You'll thank Erica Jong one day.'

Florence's face was blank as she pulled a wishbone the size of a pinky fingernail from her mouth, then set it on the side of her plate. They spent the next few minutes in silence, her grandparents noisily finishing their birds. For dessert, there were shrivelled baked apples with lowfat yogurt and some raisins in the middle.

They walked her to the door, past the MET reproduction Giacometti sculpture on the coffee table, past a first edition of Ulysses on a little stand, past the Ansel Adams print and the collection of bread plates they'd found antiquing around Rhinebeck. They bore homely slogans: 'Give Us This Day Our Daily Bread'; 'Home Sweet Home'. At the door, Carrie said, 'I wasn't sposed to mention Arnie. Please don't tell ma? Because she thinks if you know, you'll be mad. But you won't be mad, right? I think they broke up anyway.'

'Don't worry,' said her grandfather, smiling under his big grey moustache.

'It's good your mama's got one!' said her grandma, and kissed her. They gave her cab fare home, and told her to tell the elevator man to call it. But Carrie took the stairs fourteen flights down (no elevators for her – never again!), pocketed the five bucks and walked. (The cab fare-stealing was a hustle so common she and Eli had a name for it: 'Making Off Like a Bandit'.)

She walked west, passing Second Avenue, Third, Lexington, which was narrow, Madison, Park, Fifth, and then entered Central Park where – just through the entrance, in front of the closed Children's Zoo – a drunk man who had spent the day selling twisted balloons was popping his unsold wares with the lit tip of a cigarette. He offered her a dog that looked like a dick and balls. She shook her head and climbed the hill to the ring road, which she decided to take, otherwise she might end up in too isolated a spot.

Taxis with open windows flew past. Black limos with windows sealed. No buses, though; they weren't allowed on this road. This lent it – as it curved under tunnels, beside planned-out ponds, the reservoir, arbors, fields – a quieter, more suburban feel.

Carrie walked slowly beside the busy road. She was full and exhausted and oddly calm. The Arnie fuck-up hung above her like a cloud. She thought of it and then she thought, 'Fuck.' It was done. Done. What the fuck can you do?

At Tavern on the Green, nearing the West 70th exit, a gaudy white horse and buggy approached. Carrie checked to see if the horse looked healthy. Viv always made a point of commenting on the well-being of carriage horses. She had even once taken down a horse license plate number and lodged a complaint about a very skinny one. This horse looked OK.

Through the plate glass windows of Tavern on the Green, hundreds of rich people were eating their desserts. They had *frozen* hot chocolate, Helena told her, whatever that was! Just the thought of it made Carrie smile! What happiness the future held. She would have a leather briefcase and an impressive job. The kind of job Grandma Martian would brag about. A civil rights lawyer. A doctor. A husband who was *not* Lawrence Levy. As she began to detail the interior of the apartment she would occupy on Riverside Drive – the views, the 'quality pets' she would have … A man in a tuxedo jumped from the slow moving white carriage and stood in front of her, reeling like a Weeble, under a golden lamp.

His hair was short and black with a long widow's peak; his chin was pointed; his lips were red, chapped and tight with white powdery skin around them. He brandished a champagne bottle. Its gold label glittered as he held it upside down in Carrie's face and pulled her up by the collar of the Blue Snot. He lowered his peeling face to her level and stared into her eyes. His were sink drains and he smelled of vomit. He opened them wider.

'Vanity Kills, little girl! Vanity Kills! Ha ha ha ha!' He had a strange twangy accent she didn't recognize. He plunged back into the front seat of the carriage, which he was driving, and cantered off.

She kept her cool, walked to the exit of the park, and started running. She ran the rest of the avenues home, down 71st Street, Columbus, Amsterdam (well, not Amsterdam yet, the one without a name), West End. Carrie didn't care that she was afraid of elevators, and got in, panting, relieved, and ecstatic to be home.

Eli was the only one home, sitting there in his sky blue Fruit of the Looms and sweatsocks, legs crossed, on a swivel chair, grooving slightly with his Walkman on, eating a bowl of Super Sugar Crisp. Carrie pulled an earphone up and whispered loudly in his ear, 'Cornflake *game hens*.' He jumped up and pulled her ear down to his mouth as he sat back down, '*The Shining* was sold out. At fucking *MOMA*.'

Carrie took off the snot and looked in the mirror. Her hair was limp and white as Breakstones butter. Her narrow face was the color of a square five cent caramel; it was still tanned from a summer rollerskating in the park. Plus it was dirty. Her nose had a strange ball at the end of it; Viv had it too. Her arms were long and small, her neck was thin, her shoulders too high, and she'd got some stains from grandma's wet hen on Helena's red Izod. Her left ear was bright red. There was a bald patch over the right one. She had on a blue neck-lace made of baked stone that a great uncle in an old age home had sent last Christmas. It was getting to be too small, and sat too snugly around the base of her neck. There was some dirt or at least dark lines in the cracks of her lips. There were always grey-blue circles under her eyes.

Lawrence once told her they were attractive, the dark circles, 'They make you look deep, like James Dean. '

Her dad said she looked like Grace Kelly, but she did not know who that was, and he only said it when she was weeping over a dress he wouldn't buy her. Viv once said in the Southern slur that came out when she was her most drunk, 'Darlin', if you wore a potato sack they'd all be wearing one next week.' Carrie and Helena laughed about that one for months.

Eli screamed, because he had the headphones back on, and was listening to *Bridge over Troubled Water* in an attempt to console himself. 'Stop looking in the mirror! Ya vain bitch!'

'I'm gonna go out to Tony's for a Twix, you want something?'

The new *Fangoria*, if it was in.

She took the back stairs down; unlike the front stairs these had windows, and if anyone happened to come at her, to try and rape her, she could always jump. The windows were letting in the cool, high New York fall air. The wonderful soothing noises of it. Car doors closing, cars whooshing, dogs barking, laughs, whoops. When people can hear and see you, you're much safer.

'What's wrong?' asked Tony the Yemenite candy guy. His shop exuded cumin and lentils, as usual. Carrie had peeked in the back before; behind the dangerous-looking electricity/waffle cooling unit of the soda fridge there was a little windowless room with a high ceiling and thick blankets on chairs. There was always a hot plate bubbling. It always smelled divine.

'*Nada hombre.*'

Phoebe was in the back, extracting a can of Dr. Pepper

from behind some Sunkists, in the hopes that Arnie would come again. She had come to the point of admitting to herself that she *needed* someone to hear her life. But she was realistic. It was impossible to tell one person; they ran away too fast. She thought she had better tell several. If they were related, all the better. She eyed Carrie. *She* could hear the part about Lavender.

'You're Viv's daughter.'

Carrie liked her pointy shoes. They were Wizard of Oz Shoes. Red ruby slippers.

'*Te gusta mis zapatos?*'

'*Claro.*'

'You got the new *Fango*?' Carrie said to Tony.

'Yeah. Won't sell it to you, though. Your brother can come down himself.' Tony had a gold front tooth and smiled at her as he spoke.

11. What a Coinkydink

CARRIE AND PHOEBE smiled at each other outside Tony's. Across 72nd, Gristedes was still open. The dark blue letters glowed heavily. Glen the coke-dealer/meat guy was out front, laughing with a girl who was sitting on a fire hydrant. She was wearing neon-green culottes. They were smoking cigarettes. Further down the block, in front of the West End Superette, the new Mexican dude was restacking spotlit pumpkins in a tenuous pyramid. A Cadillac waited noisily, then tore through the turning lights onto the West Side Highway, home to suburban New Jersey. Carrie looked at the soft grey sidewalk, holding her Twix in her hand. She flipped it around; its foil wrapper crackled with pleasure. 'I mean, what does *he* care whether I read a horror movie magazine or not?'

'He thinks you need to be protected. Where's your briefcase?

'Oh, I don't *always* carry it. It's a security thing I guess. Some kids have blankies.'

'Do you want to come up and see my crystal ball?'

'I'd love to.'

The entrance smelled of cat piss, and it occurred to Carrie – for the first time – that maybe some *women* were to be feared. She knew about men. She paused in the small hall of Miss Rosa's apartment and didn't let the door shut; she held it open with her foot. Phoebe went and poured herself a drink.

'Why does Danny have The Shine? Is there really such a thing?' Eli had told her the whole story of *The Shining* several times. Carrie picked the Magic 8 Ball off a shelf, flipped it, closed her eyes and thought. *Q: Will I be safe here? IT IS DECIDEDLY SO*. Carrie moved her foot and let the door shut. She sat down on a stool with a blue satin seat, and crooked her head to read the titles on the lowest shelf: *The Farmer's Almanac 1915*; *The I Ching*; *The New York Times Cookbook*; *Understanding Astrology*; *Understanding Media*.

'Because it's a book.' Phoebe opened her hands, like you do to say 'book' in a game of charades. 'And a ... ' – she wound her right hand and held a invisible camera in her left – '... movie. Movies and books have to simplify and exaggerate, and leave out how much *practice* anything takes. Years and years of tedious practice, Carrie. Mark my words. I got this crystal ball in 1966 at the Woolworth's on 110th and Broadway. Like it?' She tapped the too-small ball with her pointed fingernail.

'It's very nice.'

'Eat your Twix. Come sit opposite me and listen for a little while?'

She did.

Hilda was her father's sister and had been Phoebe's 'tutor' since she was seven. In those days it was fine for girls not to go to school, as long as they learned to do needle work, and other useless things. That said, Hilda wasn't teaching Phoebe exactly what she was supposed to. When she developed breasts, for example, at 14, Hilda had insisted on feeling them everyday, and measuring them. She told Phoebe this taught about weights and measures. She even put her pupil in a tub, to test 'density' with 'water displacement.' Other topics covered were lumped under the heading 'Oriental Traditions' these included: American Indian tribes, Buddhism, the Tarot and I Ching, and spirit photography. She also taught Phoebe to cook, which *was* useful; though cooking for Hilda included lots of dissections. Hilda wouldn't eat animals, but she was fond of cutting them up.

When she was done squishing hearts and palpitating livers and eyeballs, Hilda would wrap all the parts up in an old Rhinebeck newspaper, and bring them home, to her half-brother Cyrus and his wife and kids, who lived on a shack at the top of the hill. Fondling and cutting aside, Phoebe loved Hilda. In the old days you had to spend a lot of time with people you couldn't stand.

'That still muh case.' Carrie laughed with her mouth full.

Hilda and Phoebes' parents, for example, they were dependent on each other, for food, for money, for transport, for Phoebe's education; they had to co-exist. The day Hilda offered to take Phoebe off her parents' hands – that was a great day. They were sitting at the kitchen table and Phoebe was serving potato rolls and jam. Cotton had placed Lucretia in her chair then hobbled over to his, wincing at Phoebe. *Of course* she was the one who had left the needle in the middle of the floor. Actually she'd left it sticking straight out of a cupboard, on purpose. Kids have problems, always have. The rolls were making Phoebe's parents unhappy – they wanted the rest of the chicken that was putrifying in the pantry – but the rolls were served for Hilda, out of consideration for her delicacy, her vegetarianism, which Cotton always said he had 'some sympathy with'.

'Hitler was a vegetarian. And you know what else is really weird? Carrie said enthusiastically, 'My grandparents' country house is in Rhinebeck. I'm supposed to be there right now. I was supposed to go this weekend but my dad is AWOL.'

Phoebe didn't have an appetite, and sulked by the window while the rest of them ate. Her schooling with Hilda had officially ended when she was sent to the Apthorp. She was so depressed and mortified by her failure in NYC she was actually thinking about killing herself. All along Hilda had encouraged her, told her she had 'powers'. Sometimes Phoebe even felt a little hurt, Hilda seemed so desperate for her to get out of Rhinebeck, to get to NYC.

However, watching her eat, Hilda didn't seem very disappointed. She swallowed large mouthfuls of plum jam straight off the spoon, and spun her amber and turquoise rings on her short fingers. She even smiled while Cotton and Lucretia blathered on about Farmer Morkam's exorbitant egg prices, broken gigs and Cyrus and Lucy's 'aberration.' About the aberration, they whispered.

Carrie didn't get about half of what Miss Rosa was talking about; it took a while before she even realized Phoebe was Miss Rosa – she was saying I but sometimes I in a story doesn't mean I. Besides, Carrie was congenitally self-centered and thinking the whole time about her Halloween costume. She said, 'I'm trying to get the money to buy this red devil get-up for the Halloween Parade. Have you ever been to it? In the Village? I have five bucks, but I need nine. The costume is in the window of Paper House, the uptown one. It's kind of shiny, glossy almost ...'

Phoebe said huskily, 'I'll pay you to shut up and listen.'

Carrie blushed. 'No, that's OK. I like your story.' She leaned deep into her chair.

When Hilda had eaten everything on the table, including the crumbs off everyone's plates, she tapped her knife on her tea cup.

Cotton, Lucretia and Phoebe froze like a bunch of sheep.

Hilda said, 'I'd like to employ Phoebe, Brother Cotton. Would you send her to live with me?' She never called him Brother Cotton.

Phoebe turned away and faced the stove. She had to steady herself on it. Her smile was hot like someone had slapped her.

'Please, be my guest – ' Cotton gulped his tea backwash. He never left a drop.

'*Employ*? She's utterly useless,' Lucretia finished for him, but she giggled like a schoolgirl, such was her delight.

That was the first night Phoebe met her cousin, Lavender. Before that the lessons were held strictly at The Curtises, or in the summerhouse out back. Lavender Lenape Lincoln Curtis. Which is not a funny name. It's regal, and majestic.

'Why did your parents hate you?' asked Carrie.

'I'm not sure. I think because there was too much going on between them. My father, my father was in love with one farm hand after another. It was pathetic. He was … because he had so much to hide he was very attentive to my mother, and she was … she needed a lot of attention. Who knows why! Anyway they were very close. They were best friends. I was in the way.'

'What was your house like? Ours is tiny. One bedroom for three – I mean four, if you count Arnie – people. Plus Nora and the parakeet and the gerbils and the cats.'

The Curtises lived in a grand house; picture the best house on the best street in a New England Town, and that is where Phoebe was raised – but she had never liked it. Now she was finally going to see Hilda's house, Pondweed.

When Phoebe arrived that first night, the porch was lit with tall candles. Their light danced through clumsy fret-work, poorly executed shapes: daisies, hearts and crescent moons and stars. The whitewash was peeling off the porch, and bright pink paint the color of rhododendrons showed under it. Cyrus had driven them up the hill. Phoebe had heard about him, and seen the infamous Christmas card, but she had never met him, her uncle.

'That is like so weird. My grandparent's house has hearts around it too!'

'Whereabout's the house – *in* Rhinebeck?'

'It's not *in* Rhinebeck, it's near Red Hook. It's got a shed and it's old. The kids throw their sneakers over the street lamps. It has a pond behind the hill. There's a nice brook. A babbling brook where there are salamanders and little frogs. I don't like the house, though. It's too big.'

'It's an unpleasant house.'

'You really think it's *your* old house?' Carrie was eating the second half of her Twix much more slowly than she had the first. She ate the top off first.

'Let's pretend it is. Then you can picture it better. OK? Good!'

That first night... Cyrus dropped the reins, noisily, and walked over to open the carriage door. Phoebe hadn't seen him when she got in; Hilda had helped her. He was *very* good looking, tall and wiry-thin. He had high cheekbones, reddish hair, green eyes and skin the colour of chocolate. That first night his eyes were bloodshot. They usually were. His smelled sour, of rotting corn, which is what people who drink too much homemade booze smell like, even in the morning. 'Where'd you get that scar?' That was the first thing he ever said to Phoebe. As he said it he ran his fingers over her scar.

Phoebe ran her thumb under her own old chin.

'That's *also* so weird. Arnie has that same scar! He got it from waking up a sleeping Labrador. What a coinkydink!'

'Let sleeping dogs lie, that's the truth. Even Nora.'

Hilda rushed up behind Cy when he touched Phoebe, and pulled his ear to her mouth. She was a full foot shorter than him, but she pinched him hard. 'Get back to your place and take care of your own, brother.' She said. Phoebe was aghast. She had never seen Hilda act that way. Hilda was beaming wildly. Cyrus pulled himself loose of her grip and walked a few paces backwards towards his shack, a vaguely glimmering place on top of the hillock. He cackled, 'You got a great grip.'

'Holy fucking shit, that shack's still there!'

'Course it is, *it is* the same house. It sounds like a crazy place, I guess. I guess it was. It was awful, too, but I was – I don't know – just so goddamned *relieved* to finally be there.'

'I know what you mean.' Carrie yawned. Her Twix was history. 'I have this thing where … when I'm with grown ups I don't know, like a friend's parents, and we're eating dinner, or shopping, anything – I get so pissed off! I want to hide or run away and scream. People want you to be boring. My ma's not like that. You're not like that. What was it like inside Hilda's house? Was it beautiful? I see candles and heavy drapes, and mirrors and silver plates, and gold plates.'

'The silver apples of the moon. The golden apples of the sun. Yes, that's *exactly* what it was like.'

Hilda had made Phoebe's room up in advance, she must have been confidant her offer wouldn't be refused. Phoebe got into bed, but she couldn't sleep, so she went downstairs in the half-attached corset she had been wearing for two days. Hilda stared at her. Also in a new way. She'd been reading in a rocking chair – *The Farmer's Almanac* – wearing her pince-nez. Phoebe wasn't a shy girl; she sat down on the floor and leaned against the wall. Hilda went back to reading, or pretending to, and Phoebe picked up a statue of a black boy – a stand, really – a black boy, holding a plateful of fruit, with a tray on his head for your drink. A blackamoor. Huge red lips and no pupils, only white eyes.

'Holy holy fucking fucking shitshit! It *is* the house. My grandparents still have that blackamoor! They claim it's worth a lotta money. Or would be but it has a dent in it.'

'Of course it is. We agreed on that. We made a pact, Carrie. *It is the same house.*'

Phoebe looked at Carrie hard for a minute, and a light came into her eyes that had not been there in decades. A light that connected her to people. Such a beautiful, rapturous light. Then it went out.

On the wall there was a hand-drawn family tree in the shape of a weeping willow. Hilda's name, highlighted in gold filigree, dangled at the tip of a branch, in the shape of a catkin. Hilda said that one of Cyrus's sons, Lavender, had drawn it. She stood and led Phoebe down the hall and into a darkened bedroom. In the moonlight Phoebe saw his little body, under a warm blanket, moving with his breath. He was glowing. Back in the hall Hilda whispered that she thought Lavender was the reincarnation of an African king or Indian Chief. Phoebe felt different at Pondweed, free for the first time in her life, and she spoke up. She told Hilda what a load of bullshit she thought reincarnation was, but she admitted, he seemed unearthly.

'You don't believe in reincarnation? I do,' said Carrie.

'You think you were Cleopatra in your past life?'

'You never know.'

'I'll stop. You look tired. Go.'

Carrie did. On the way out she thought of saying 'goodnight', the way people did in movies, but it seemed ostentatious. She couldn't think of how to say anything, so she just closed the door.

Phoebe sat in her chair, under her neon rose and backwards stencils.

Carrie's leaving was so sudden. Endings *were* sudden. Unless you intentionally dragged them out. She listened to the street. Telling the story had set a loneliness climbing, starting at her ankles, growing up her legs, like a weed.

12. We're on the 11 o'clock News!

ARNIE WAS HIDEOUSLY lonely. Ever since he met Lucy he'd felt lonelier and lonelier when they were apart. It worried him. He made an attempt to get her out of his head, or to dump Viv, or maybe to just stir shit up, he wasn't sure. *Let's go out, Mrs Robinson*, he'd sung to Viv, when he got home from Lucy's.

On the street people looked at Viv and Arnie like she *was* Mrs Robinson, and he was a cuter Dustin Hoffman – no, that other guy – what's his name? – Jon Voight? Jon Voight. Viv's the one who attracts attention, though. Something about her carriage. It's the Tai Chi. Her back is straight, her arms have weight, her *energy is centered*. They walked east to Swiss Chalet BBQ for bad soul food. The sidewalk was too crowded. Columbus was a dark carnival with acres of milling tourists in from Jersey, so Viv and Arnie walked fast in the road with horse cabs off the Plaza, taxis, and limos. He's a local now. And a grown-up. With problems. Two women. One older than his mom. The young one seems together, *too* together, too grown up. He'd like to knock her down a peg. Gently.

Outside the Dakota a handful of John Lennon mourners were camped out.

'*Imagine* – it's been two years and they're still there.'

They'd smoked a joint and Viv was famished. She was copper from lying on the roof all summer smothered in Ban de Soleil, a paper plate covered in tin foil under her face. A woman ten years her junior who thought Viv looked cool, a reporter in a trench coat and trench-coat-colored lipstick, summoned her television crew. Big camera; fuzzy orange boom; lop-sided hunchbacked cameraman. The microphone dropped into Viv's face. In the frame, the cameraman had the white bricks of the 40-storey hi-rise beside the Dakota, and the gold script on the deep black awning of the Swiss Chalet marquis.

'Would you be willing to answer a few questions about the abortion? … Shit. Sorry. Can we take that again. Sorry folks just a sec.'

Roll sound, speed, action.

'Would you be willing to answer a question about abortion?'

Viv glowed under her tan, 'There is no question – it's a woman's choice. It's not a public issue. It's a private issue.' Arnie put a hand on her shoulder and cracked a shit-eating grin. He's never been on TV before.

Awaiting drinks at Swiss Chalet, from the phone box outside the downstairs toilet where he'd snorted three large lines of not very good coke (cut with too much lanacane, a baby laxative) Arnie called Lucy. Answering machine. He closed his eyes and pictured it on her bedside table. The initial clicks; the double tapes spinning; its pleasant machine smell. 'Where rocking-horse people eat looking-glass pies,' said Arnie, along with other misremembered lyrics. Then he hung up. And mumbled *I love you* after he had. He smelled her on him in the close phone box. He was really far gone.

Over dinner Arnie and Viv argued about abortion. Arnie didn't argue very well. His only refutation was, 'I'm not so sure about that.' Viv said there was no moral question, no question of anyone 'dying'. It was only practical, it was only the mom's choice. Viv had had to have an abortion after the second time she was raped, and it had gone fine, her illegal abortion (but many women had died in those days, before *he* was born). 'You can't make someone bake a loaf of bread; it's no one's business,' she'd said drunkenly, then ordered another Piña in a glass the size of a salad bowl.

Arnie and Viv hurried home through the thinning crowds

of 72nd. Viv was worried they'd miss themselves on the news, even though it wasn't going to be on for a half an hour. One of her quirks was that she was always early, always over-prepared; it was a remnant of her pre-pot days, her student council-delegate days. Once they were in the lobby, Arnie decided to try Lucy again, from the payphone across the street; he said he needed some Alka and would be back in ten. Viv barely noticed he was gone.

Upstairs she arranged herself on the orange loveseat, kicked her Adidas off, suffered the end of the *Love Boat* and the long stretch of commercials that led up to the 11 o'clock news. She had a lot of digesting to do: a rack of pork ribs and half a chicken. Viv ate in quantity about once a week – the rest of the time she picked at everyone else's scraps. She didn't notice Elijah on the swivel chair until she'd been in for ten minutes. He glowered.

'You're sloshed.'

'No ah ain't, sugar.'

Carrie came back from Rosa's.

'They didn't have your magazine but Tony said no anyway. You'll have to get it. He thinks it will corrupt me.'

They all watched the news in its entirety. There was a long Health Special about AIDS. Viv intoned southernly, 'I've had three friends who've dahd this year. One dahd of chicken pox, which ain't normal. I'm sho' that's what it was. It destroys yo' immune system. God help us.'

'How do you get it, could I have it?' Carrie was worried.

'No ya yutz,' said Eli. 'Shit, wait – didn't you have anal sex and share a hypodermic needle with those friends of Arnie's we met? You're screwed.'

The abortion story had been cut. They watched the depressing news beginning to end: no mom. Then *The Honeymooners* came on, Eli and Carrie went to their divided room and Viv opened the couch bed. From the phone box across the street Arnie left another message on Lucy's machine, then went to Miss Rosa. He forgot about the news.

He shook Phoebe awake.

'Christ, *what*? Six dollars, discount.'

Arnie was coming down off coke, hungry and sad and drunk still on the Piñas. He spoke softly and ran his hands over his face and through his hair. 'I don't know how to leave her. Miss Rosa?'

Phoebe raised her head off the table but left her arms flat; she looked like a tortoise. 'Name's Phoebe, not Rosa. Just leave her. Go with the black girl your own age. It makes sense. Viv'll be ok. Get outta here. Can't you see I'm sleeping?'

Arnie started opening her couch bed. 'You can't sleep on the table. What about the kids? What about Carrie?'

'Those kids are finished.' She let him lead her to her sofa bed. She lay in it and pulled the patchwork quilt over her head.

Arnie played with a blob of red wax he'd picked off a burning candle, and looked in the mirror over the mantle. His face seemed tragic and handsome in the streetlight. Long shadows made his cheekbones higher, his eyes hollower, his hair a ghostly grey. He wanted to run off to Mexico with Lucy, the way fugitives do in movies after they shoot someone by mistake. Lucy would have a scarf tied around her head and cat-shaped sunglasses on. They'd be driving a '56 Chevy Convertible. Arnie would be in a bomber jacket. 'Have you ever been out of the U.S.?' he asked.

'I've never been outta NY State.'

'I'm starving.' He opened the knee-high refrigerator, 'I couldn't eat. I'm on so much coke. I've done an eight-ball myself. I kept calling Lucy. I wanted to share it with her. Viv's against coke, all of a sudden. Says it makes her want to puke. Fuck. Viv had ribs and onion rings. And chicken. And corn bread. And three Piñas. And onion rings. Wish I had some *now*.'

'You said onion rings twice.' Phoebe was under the covers. She had never been under the covers while someone went through her refrigerator.

'They're great. You get a whole big pile. It's called a *loaf*. All you have in here is sour cream.'

'I love sour cream. It's great. It's good on its own. It's good on everything. Why are you on coke all the time?'

'I think it's addictive.'

'Let me quickly tell you a little about him. It'll take five minutes?'

'Who?'

'Lavender. Little boy I knew. He was … Lemme tell you a little? Just before I fall asleep.'

He looked worried but sat down with the sour cream and a teaspoon. 'OK, Phoebe. Shoot.'

The first few weeks Hilda wanted Phoebe all the time; she'd waited years, and Phoebe would oblige, but only at night. In the day, Phoebe looked through every room in Pondweed, opening and closing books, opening drawers and trunks, examining swords and shrunken heads, gold rings and leather helmets, carved Buddhas and rabbit's feet. There were fifteen rooms in Hilda's dead parents' farmhouse, all crammed. Phoebe's grandfather and Hilda's dad, Lear Curtis, had gone mad from syphilis, but before that he had collected huge amounts: booze, guns, books, taxidermal things. Like the rest of her life Phoebe could recall any moment perfectly; of all her days she could tell you facts, prices, words, but those months at Pondweed – she could still *feel*.

Hilda would begin the day trying to find Phoebe – she wanted more than the nights – but Hilda was lazy, spoiled and stout; by noon she'd be on the porch, smoking pot out of a pipe, her feet up. Phoebe would only be a quarter of the way through her rummaging – often in the company of Lavender Lenape. (Lavender was the only child Cyrus' wife Lucy would allow to spend time with the Pondweed crew.) She and Lavender made up stories about the things they found, and cleaned them off, and put them back.

One day Phoebe, Cyrus, Hilda and Lavender were out in a

field joining in some Byrdcliffe summer solstice celebration. Byrdcliffe? Byrdcliffe was basically, a proto-hippie community near where they lived, but it was too serious for the likes of them. They were just there for the food, and to look at the girls, who believed in free love. Anyway, everyone was required to be barefoot. Hilda and Cyrus' feet were exactly the same: rectangular and flat and long. Cyrus' were dark and ashy, Hilda's pink and filthy as a pig's.

Cyrus and Hilda were arguing and giggling and kicking each other; they were supposed to be doing a potato sack race, and were high out of their minds – which was almost always the case. No, it wasn't illegal then. Cyrus grew it next to the sunflowers; he was very good in the garden, he knew all about what flowers and crops grew well together. He dried it in the loft of his shack. The marijuana. Lucy hated it. She wouldn't touch it. All poor Lucy did was read the Bible.

Cyrus had a thing about purity. He had to think women (except Hilda) were better people than men. His mom had been a bit of a bad seed, and had died when he was young. She'd been a quarter-Lenape, a quarter-daughter-of-a-slave, and half-slave owner, and by all accounts a very angry and very clever woman. She and Lear Curtis were quite the pair, cinematic in their good looks and evil deeds. There were rumours they did things to children. But Cyrus would hear nothing of it. As far as he was concerned the light shined out of his dead mother's ass, and his father was Mr Johnson, the dark-eyed, near-silent farm hand she had been married to – and who was, incidentally, Cotton Curtis' first love. But even though Cyrus screwed any woman who would, and was a drunk, he never said a word against Lucy, and in the shack he was the same.

They already had six kids when Phoebe left. Well, five. Lucy felt it was her wifely duty to have sex with Cy whenever he wanted, and he was a very horny guy.

'Just like you, Arnie.'

Arnie went 'Hmmm,' unamused, frowning.

Hilda would sleep with Cy about once a month, when she was blacked-out drunk, and he came inside her; but she never got pregnant. Maybe she couldn't. He came inside her because she begged him to! Then she never wanted to hear about it. It was the only time you saw her blush. She'd covered her ears and stamp her foot: 'Stop. Please stop!' Cyrus wouldn't quit: 'That's not what you was saying last night, Lordy no. Tell her Miss Phoebe.' Phoebe would join in: 'I couldn't sleep for the howlin', Aunt.'

They called each other niece and aunt, and Hilda and Phoebe called Cyrus brother and uncle – but Cyrus wouldn't call Phoebe niece or Hilda sister, because he believed they weren't related. It doesn't sound funny but they'd laugh and laugh as they called to each other. They might be sitting on the porch at sunset facing the valley, which had a green mist over it, getting high. Phoebe would be braiding Lavender's hair in rows. He had beautiful hair. Smooth and soft as rose petals – when Lucy hadn't got her hands on it. The things Lucy put in his hair, the stinky oils and tonics to make it 'more white'.

'This is all *really* to my liking, the sex stuff, the incest stuff. And the pot! Wish I had some. You don't have any do you? God I feel like shit. Fuck, I gotta go see if we're on the 11 o'clock News. Shit. Forgot. Some chick asked Viv about abortion. I need to know about this little girl I met: Lucy. Can you tell me? What does she think of me? Can I … can I have her?' Arnie wiped a tear off his cheek: coke-hangover. Really fun. *Immediate*.

The neon rose flickered and changed the room. It flickered for a half a minute; the clown's greatcoat changed with it, making small rainbow shadows on the wall behind it, and then it was grey. The rose went dead. A detail changed in hundreds of peoples' views.

'Well that's *that*. *C'est fini*,' she said. She only knew from the sound.

'I wanted to know. I dunno,' Arnie was already in the front hall. 'What you think Lucy really thinks of me?' Arnie put his hand on the doorknob.

'*Is it not funny* that you're here about a girl called Lucy, and I'm telling you about a woman called Lucy?'

'Not *that* funny.' He was crying again. He decided he'd quit coke.

'And isn't it funny that Viv is going off for an abortion, and I'm about to tell you this part of the story where Lucy – the same name as the black girl you're in love with, and why not picture her exactly the same way, why not, what's to stop you, really? – almost dies, from a really bad one. I think it's *funny*.' Phoebe laughed.

Arnie stood where he was for a second, said, *motherfucker*, then pulled the door shut behind him. Because although it was obvious, he hadn't noticed Viv was.

That was a bad time. Lucy's abortion. After Lavender she said – *no more*. God was punishing her with Lavender, she thought. In those days, well in *those* days, you didn't just go around the corner for an abortion. The Curtis' neighbor, the town doctor, performed them on white ladies, but no one was going to give one to Lucy. Hilda made pennyroyal tea by the bucket, but it didn't work. Finally they had to pack Cyrus and Lucy off to Baltimore. They found a black doctor through an ad in the back of the paper. He advertised as a 'specialist in automatic writing', which someone at Byrdcliffe told them, was code for abortionist. Aren't codes odd. Like those sneakers they hang over the tree by Carrie's grandparents. They mean *drugs are sold here*. It *is* the same house. On Pumpkin Lane. It was called Nine Partners Road then. Pumpkin Lane, what an absurd name! So Cy took her up there in the gig. They were a pathetic sight. Cy in his shabby Sunday suit and sad face. Lucy's as sallow as a NYC seagull, dreading the two-day ride alongside fast carriages and cars; and her sin too, of course. When he got her home she was half dead, bleeding pints and pints. They put her in Hilda's featherbed. They made ginger tea and garlic tea and she drank it, and they rubbed salves on her. No penicillin.

Phoebe was under the covers. Seeing things. She didn't know if she had been speaking, or thinking.

One night, when it looked like she was going to die, she asked to see Lavender. He came out crying. He said she told him she couldn't bear to bring another monster into God's great and perfectly-formed world, and that was why she was nearly dead; she explained her abortion to him. The she made him lay his hand on her Bible and swear he'd cut it off when he was old enough. He was five. But then ... Lucy started to get better. And Phoebe thought – no, Phoebe *knew* it was his oath that brought Lucy through.

Lavender had both. It's not as rare as you think, actually. He was lovely. Just a lovely little kid. A gift from God, if ever there was one.

13. Mr. Murray Martian the Ascetic and his Unbreakable Plate

MONDAY, THERE WAS no school, thank God: it was Columbus Day Holiday, so Eli and Carrie had to stay on their own and, as Viv put it, 'amuse themselves'. First thing in the morning, after their mom left for Macy's, Carrie went out to get some red thread to sew the tail on her Red Devil Costume. Woolworth's on 69th only had maroon. She bought it, which left $4.39 from the bandit cabfare for her costume. On the way home she saw her reflection in the window of Off Track Betting. She was bent forward, almost in half, in her A-shaped green polyester skirt. She looked so weird. So rushed.

Panting from the run up the stairs, she pushed the door open. Eli was still in his bed. Arnie wasn't there. Carrie started picking things up off the floor and putting them on the table. She cleaned, because the room wasn't separate enough from her: if she saw disorder *she* was disorder. She swept up dog hair, dry roasted peanuts and bits of plastic toys. From the odds and ends she chose two things to add to her *attaché*: a plastic bead and the small head of a female action figure. She turned on the TV. *It's The Great Pumpkin, Charlie Brown* was being replayed from last night. It felt like a gift from some beneficent deity. Carrie dropped the broom and sat down in front of the TV with a plate that had a high edge (she was using it as a bowl) full of Honeycombs with strawberries on top.

A couple of hours later Viv and her ex-father-in-law Mr Murray Martian were having an early lunch at the Four Seasons.

'O, Lord' said Murray Martian loudly. He'd ordered the steak tartar. Viv was having Caesar salad and two Beefeater martinis.

'The kids love him and it's free baby-sitting.' This was the best Viv could come up with in defense of having a nineteen-year-old live-in boyfriend. It's a wonder she hadn't worked in *three* places called the Self Center.

Mr Martian had a Diner's Club coupon. He told Viv that they were entitled to a glass of house red or white, *but no:* she had to have martinis. Viv had taken the afternoon off work and wasn't about to waste it. On the way over to meet her, Murray had found himself running ten minutes early, so he stopped to try on hats in the Stetson shop. His head was too small for most of them; he was six foot three with a head the size of a ten-year-old. One hat fit: wide-brimmed, white felt, with a tan band. He fretted, asking the salesgirl a lot of questions about where it came from and how it was made. After ten minutes he decided against it and said 'I'd never keep it clean. I'd manage to get mustard on it.' She didn't smile. She was wearing two pins, Sid Vicious and Elvis, on opposite lapels.

'It's ironic you know, because he's moving out. I'm pretty sure.' Viv impaled an anchovy on a tin and swizzled her fork between her thumb and forefinger, twirling it. She chewed on an olive from her martini. She was very impressed with the pastel and metallic decor. She felt like she was in a movie. Something with Meryl Streep as a flustered working mother.

Murray ignored her comment and stared at the anchovy, wishing he had bought the hat. 'Well, he might contribute something to the rent. I mean – look Vivian, Ethan should be doing it, but for whatever reason... Florence and I, we both think it's time you pulled a little more of your own weight. If you'd stayed in Santa Cruz' – where Ethan had had an assistant professorship in Philosophical Logic – 'you'd own a house by now. The kids would be settled, in school. Maybe there'd be more of you.'

Viv snorted at the thought of the embryo. Then, drunk, thought she had a great idea. 'They *are* settled, *in school*. That reminds me: Carrie was asking the other day about money for boarding school. She's been writing this application essay. She's dying to get away from NY for some reason. Oh and there's another thing. There's another thing. I'm pregnant.' She snorted again. 'Can you lend me some money for the abortion? It's 500 dollars.' She finished her second martini and couldn't look at him. Even for her, this move was a bit much.

He spoke quietly but without feeling. 'That private? The clinics are just fine. Harold runs the one on 100th and 3rd. I can get you in there. With him.'

'OK.'

Mr Martian smiled and played with his moustache and asked for the bill by raising his eyebrows. Then he started rabbiting on about the Nietzsche he'd been reading. He said the difference between the Blonde Beast and the Ascetic was vital to understanding ownership. 'The Blonde Beast,' he explained – as Viv mini-pirate-sworded her second olive, got it in her mouth, and tried to lap the gin out of it with the tip of her tongue – 'has a sense of entitlement, whereas the Ascetic has a sense of resentment.' Him? Murray? He never thought he deserved anything, so he worked extra hard.

They parted amicably, heading off into the drizzle in opposite directions. Murray went and got himself the hat, reasoning that it was only so often one 'falls in love with an object'. Viv walked home, four miles, by way of Central Park. Men looked at her. She was going to be forty-one soon. She knew there would be at least a hundred less in the bank next month. What was odd about the way she walked is she didn't shrink from the rain, didn't hunch her shoulders, or hold her camouflage coat closed over her chest. She strutted through the city, calculating how much money she would have to live on. And it was so little that she snorted a third time.

Uptown, Carrie bet Eli the $4.39 that he would not have the nerve to go down to Miss Rosa's. Carrie wanted Eli out of her hair so she could watch the end of good-hearted Charlie Brown in peace. She had started out with offering three bucks, but he pushed for all the remaining 'bandit'. He was terrified of Miss Rosa.

'You're chickenshit!'

'She is the wrong color. Her skin is the color of Silly Puddy. She has *applied* her skin. She's a witch, I tell you!'

'Come on – we've all been in her lair. You have to. Or you're no Martian.'

Eli went. It took ten minutes for the elevator to show. When he was getting out, he pressed all the buttons so whoever needed it next would have to wait as long as he had.

He stood in Phoebe's hall and said, 'I'm only here to get $4.39. Carrie bet me I wouldn't last half an hour.'

Phoebe was in bed. She'd been out to buy cigarettes and some sour cream but she'd crawled back under the blanket. She was surprised how much she liked it under there, the heat of her own breath. She'd decided she was retired.

'OK kiddo. I'll pick up where I left off. Have you heard what I've been telling Arnie and Carrie and Viv? They can fill you in.'

They thought about joining the Byrdcliffe community. Cyrus was a strong supporter; he thought they should buy a loom and join up. Think of the women! And they adored *him*, the Byrdcliffians. Maybe because he was black, which made it quite radical. And he would have been an asset. He was a very good farmer. He used to set the gramophone up by the window and play music to his corn.

'My ma has a record, Music to Grow Plants By,' said Eli, very nervously.

Hilda was more practical, though, she objected to the fees, and she didn't want to leave her house or let a bunch of strangers move in and turn Pondweed into a commune. Phoebe was so young she was neutral. Actually, then, as now, not much got to her. Maybe because she saw everything? Who knows. This was around the time Freudian analysis was erupting. The cause of *everything* was sexual repression. If you burnt the potatoes it was a sign of sexual frustration. They played around – with séances, with automatic writing, Tarot, spirit pictures, orgies … and the Byrdcliffians were not really on that wavelength. All they did was make stained glass and yogurt.

'Come here, boy.' Phoebe stuck her head out from under the covers, but the room still looked very dark. She made out Eli's podgy form. She had lost her eyesight; it only occurred to her at that moment. I know what you're thinking: impossible: you would notice. But you might not. She had stopped moving around because of pain, and the pain had increased, it was in her … *seat*, that's the best way to describe it, the place that had kept her too-rooted to her psychic's chair. But though the pain had gotten worse, she had changed the extent to which she experienced it; she had shifted up, and experienced all physical sensation less. It was the same with seeing. She'd been living in very dim light for almost thirty years. For the ambiance, for the depth of the shadows, for the muted, mutable colors that are lost in bright sun and electric light. Candles bring a filter to a world. They impose themselves, like any good medium. So, no: she had not noticed she was practically blind until that very moment.

Eli stayed in the hall, pretending to read *The Farmers Almanac 1915*. Then he flipped the Magic 8 Ball and mouthed, 'Is she a witch?' IT IS DECIDEDLY SO.

Eli asked her if she had seen *Hair*.

'Do I look like I've seen *Hair*?'

'In it these Hippies, they try to dodge the draft – and in the end, it's ironic because after all that the guy ends up going to the war and he dies. Weird, right?'

'Come *here*,' She stuck her finger out from under the cover and curled it at him, 'Wanna know the scariest thing that ever happened to me?'

'*Hell* no.'

'You still have twenty minutes if you want the $4.39.'

Phoebe saw a red room that she did not recognize, one she couldn't remember. It was a room with a Christmas tree jammed in the corner, its tip shoved right up into the ceiling. A round threadbare rug on the floor. Grey-yellow light pouring through slatted windows. There was a fifteen year-old girl in yards and yards of mohair poodle skirt and high spectator heels, her legs crossed, her back concave as she leaned way over a Life Magazine, reading, chewing earnestly on a pen. Phoebe could not see what the article was that so engrossed her. She recognized Viv though, by her ears, and said to Eli: 'When your mother was 22 she went out one night. It was autumn, around this time of year.'

'Is this about when she spent the night in the haunted house? Then found out that guy hung, sorry – I always get that wrong – *hanged*, himself there?'

'Nope.'

'Oh. What?' Eli was thinking she wasn't so bad. She knew how to talk to him. He made his way to the sink, a few steps into the ex-ballroom.

Phoebe heard herself speaking in a too-low voice. 'Here, I'll tell you. Your mother, all her clothes taken but her high-heeled go-go boots, getting fucked by one man in the ass and another in the mouth, with her face like the Mona Lisa, because she was not there. She was not observing. She was not a spectator. I tell you, so you can start to understand the difference between scary things in real life and those in the movies.'

Eli looked at the tops of his sneakers and walked backwards six steps and spat very quietly on the floor first on

117

his left and then on his right. This was part of a spell to keep witches away that he saw on an after school special. He said, 'John over John' and 'John the Conqueror' as he walked.

Phoebe knew all about John the Conqueror root. A witch! She wished! She, pulled the cover off, and opened her eyes so wide they felt like would pop out. All she saw was a liquid blob, which *really* pissed her off. Blind! She threw the fifth of booze that sat on her end table against the wall and it broke and left an orange stain with streaks that went *up*.

'Get out!' she screamed. 'I had to tell *you* that. Can't you understand *anything*? Kids these days. So *stupid* ...' She was still blubbering when he shot down the stairs and out the door and into the great, welcoming NY wet, into its huge white arms.

Carrie looked up from the TV. Eli turned the knob OFF. 'Yo! What the fuck!' slurped Carrie, who was on her fourth plate of Honeycombs.

'She is a fucking witch and no one' – Eli was shaking, halving a pot seed he'd picked up off the table, rolling it madly in his sweaty fingers – 'NO ONE is going back there.'

Carrie rolled her eyes, 'I can go there if I fucking want. I like her.'

She picked up the application to boarding school off the floor. It was so smooth and stiff; nothing had been written on it. This was escape plan M. At one point last year she had actually spent two afternoons in the library researching defecting to the Soviet Union. Ethan was a Marxist. But this: this made sense. If only she didn't suck at spelling. She couldn't spell her way out of a paper bag.

Eli came over and grabbed her hair and shook her by it.

'Get the fuck off of me!' She had not seen this coming. She should have.

'Say you won't go back there.'

'I'll fucking go back there if I fucking want you fucking dick.'

118

Eli picked up the square green plastic 'unbreakable' plate half-full of sodden Honeycombs (the plates were a gift from the Martians after they'd bought a new set of dishes, as was their wont; they redecorated every so often, just for the hell of it) and threw it against the wall, where it broke in several large shards and left jellyfish-like clumps of cereal on the wall. She did not go limp. Carrie had perfected the most ergonomic posture in which to have your hair pulled. You give in, but you hold your head steady.

'Say you won't go. That's all I'm fucking asking.' Eli was crying, snot running down his face and into his mouth.

Carrie screamed 'FUCK YOU FUCK YOU FUCK YOU FUCK YOU FUCK YOU!' in a crescendo that upset the naked old people across the courtyard.

(Arnie was in bed with Lucy on Lexington and 95th. They were having a post-coital chat. Arnie was sweetly telling her he wanted to have her child. Lucy was sweetly crying about Viv's pregnancy. Lucy had been brought up a Christian, and she still wore a tiny gold cross. Sexy! Viv was down at Goodbar's, having her fourth martini of the day, playing the Beach Boys and talking to Phil Silver about his love life. Viv hardly ever talked about her problems. They embarrassed her. She felt they were her fault, a failing, a wrong-color stitch in a seamless scene.)

'Pick it up, bitch.'

Eli banged her head against the wall, kicked her in the ribs and pushed her under the table.

Carrie wanted to get closer to the back door in the kitchen, so she crawled further under the table and kicked the plate-pieces out. Then she stayed still for a moment, as if exhausted. She knew how long it would be before his guard went. About 100 seconds. Once you passed the minute mark he got confused, but if you stayed *too* long, he thought you weren't taking this seriously enough. At 100, she bolted – out the back door – and flew down the back stairs, taking four steps at a time, bounding around the corners on each landing, knocking her knees off the walls.

Carrie didn't know how she knew to look in at Goodbar's – but there was Viv. 'Oh Ma!'

Viv was in the corner, sucking her olive. 'Sugar?' She had a Southern accent.

* * *

The next day, after school, Carrie went round to Miss Rosa's to avoid being in the house with Eli.

'It's my fault.' Phoebe said, 'He's a piece of shit, your brother. Maybe he isn't even your brother. Your dad one?'

'Yeah. Well... sort-of.' Carrie looked like she was thinking about it, 'Not really, actually. He's nice. Anyway it hurts Eli more than it hurts me. He's a total asshole.'

The downstairs buzzer rang. 'Oh – that's my ma!'

Viv was great hungover; her sugar balanced, for once. She was picking Carrie up from The Psychic (they all called her that now, finding the two-names-thing too confusing, and unable to remember which one Phoebe found offensive). They were going to walk uptown, and Viv was going to borrow money from her old friend Johnny Madrid at the flower shop he owned. He still thought Viv was the ultimate woman. Determined by the times, yes, but woman through and through. Viv didn't care either way. She could take having no pot today (day one) with a hangover – her head flooded with a pleasant fog, like a Cape Cod dawn remembered – but she *could not* face tomorrow, back to her almost-real self. 'Some people just like to alter their perception,' she told Carrie on their way uptown. Carrie eyed the gargoyles on the buildings on Riverside Drive: dusty, painted black, corroded, with wrinkled looming brows and puckered lips. She swung her attaché up and down and all the way round and over her head. Viv continued. 'It's a personal preference. Like whether you're straight or gay.'

That set Carrie wondering if she would be gay. His father's roommate Daisy was. She was pretty and happy and had a good job working for the Board of Education, and she always took them out to health food restaurants when her father didn't feed them.

When they got home with the money, Eli wouldn't unlock the door because they had not brought any food. There was nothing in the house. Even the 'emergency' can of Broadcast Hash was gone. The only way to get in was to agree to take him to McDonald's.

After a slight chill in the atmosphere had gone, the usual french fry-length competition. 'Mom, whose is longer?!' 'Mom whose is longer?!' 'Mom whose is –'

'Ugh. Jeez! I'm not playing this any more.' She'd already blown 8 of the 40 bucks Johnny had lent her.

Viv ate her burger in the blink of an eye and stood up with her hands on her hips and watched the kids slurp their chocolate shakes. She ate discarded pickles off the tracing paper wrappers. It was always so cold in McDonald's; when you went out into the city the air felt cosy as a quilt, warm and muffled and welcoming. God, she loved NY!

'I do think fall is New York's best season!' she said to the kids, cheerily, as they walked home along 71st.

14. Daisy's Fingers

THE FALL AIR felt wonderful; cool and warm at once. Carrie was drafting the essay section of her boarding school application on paper plates, and was leaning the plate on the window ledge in the kitchen while watching the traffic on 71st. A white van opened and closed a door. A man put a stack of papers tied with a bow on the sidewalk, then drove off. Why the bow? Two kids had a race all the way to the corner, and then around the block. She watched them touch the ground, crouch to start, then shoot off...

If accepted I will endeaeavor to become a well known veterinarian. I already know a great deal about dogs. My dog Nora is whats known as norotic

When I grow up

My mother and father take a lot of drugs. On the margins of society one

Today I came home and stared cleaning. I cleaned and I cleaned but when I turned around I saw more to do. I When I looked in the closet it made me soooo tired just looking at it that I went and stood at the window . It seemed idel to stand three so I made myself count the number of windows I could see. I got up to 900. My favorite window isn't a window. its really what they call a french door that opens onto a orange terrace 9 stories down for me. I've seen the man who lives there water his tomooe plants day after day, year after year. He eats them on the terace in the summer with his shirt off and his flabby gut exposed. He balences the bowl of tomaoes and lettuce and he lies back in his beach chair and takes in the rays. In the fall he moves the plants inside the door, and does not come out much. I think he does not move around in cold weather, like a tortoise. In his apartment he sits down alone everynight to a rich and complex meal by candlelight.

As I stand in my window and look out I absorb things and I make things up. The light, other people. Or I geuss its only a guess as to what I am absorbing, but something comes over me. I am not sure what this means but it is the best part of my day. More important than homework (which I enjoy) or reading (which I also like very much). This time of reflection is

Grabbing a new plate, she saw it was already written on, and had been shuffled back mid-stack. In Viv's large flowing script, somehow more like a rubber stamp than handwriting, Carrie read:

How do you think about abortion without being sentimental?

Phoebe told me to be smart and abort. Phoebe is a veritable old bag.

The door opened. Arnie stuck his head in. 'Your ma here?'

Carrie put down her disposable fountain pen and frisbeed the paper plates out the kitchen window (she had the cat screen out). She watched them fly like big snowflakes in a strong wind, circling down, down, down into the courtyard. Then she quickly and clumsily put the screen back in, and shook it to make sure it was secure.

'Nuh uh.'

'I'm getting my stuff. I'm moving in with Lucy. It's just crosstown. I'm being transferred to the Gristedes on Bleeker Street! It's a great place. You can come visit me there and

I'll give you free Dr. Peppers and Doritos. *Under Gristedes, Gristedes! When the sun goes down they take the coke out of the baggie, and cut a big fat line that makes you think you brain is waterproof!...'* He was throwing things into a yellow plastic Gristedes bag with its blue silhouette of the skyline.

Carrie started singing loudly over him, 'I hate Dr. Pepper, don't ya know!'

'Ok, Perrier and Cheetos. They still your favorite?'

In no time Arnie had packed his Gristedes bag with: disposable razors, a half-used bar of Dial, neck ties, work shirts and underwear. He left out the back door, the door which was so heavy, and closed so slowly. It was structurally incapable of making a sound when it shut. Many had tried to slam it; all had failed.

Eli came in the front door right as Arnie left out the back. Carrie felt like she was in a sit-com someone had forgot to make funny. 'He's *moving out.*' She was still singing. This to the Billy Joel tune.

'Mom is pregnant.' Eli took off his headphones and threw his backpack on the floor. Then he said, 'I'm starving. She'll just vacuum it. Anyway aren't we are supposed to go meet dad at the rehearsal space?'

'I don't want to. It makes me go deaf. It's a windowless doorless cat box.' Carrie stared out the window, mournfully chewing on the cap of her fountain pen. Maybe it wasn't such a good idea to just chuck the plates out: one had hooked itself on nothing, and was flat against a low wall opposite.

'Thank you, John Ass -berry. He's gonna take us out to eat. We're gonna meet his new girlfriend, French Gil.'

'Why didn't you *say* we were going out to eat!'

On the subway on the way downtown (Viv had left the cab fare, but they – or more precisely Eli – had 'made off like a bandit'), Carrie kept chewing on the pen. It was a freebee from Murray, and it probably said Ladies Home Journal Like One Million Years on it. Eli was writing notes in his copy of *The Shining*. After 50th Street Eli turned to Carrie and said, 'You have ink, like, all over your fucking face.' And started laughing.

It ran down her chin. It soaked both her hands. People stared, which made them laugh so hard they had to stamp their little feet to keep from peeing.

From the 28th Street station it was a non-existent walk to 152 West 28th. They buzzed and waited, then the door opened to a sound of somewhere else on the intercom, but no voice. Another buzz let them into the elevator with its shiny red plastic walls. They waited again for their father to 'call it up.' The third button press. The crucial one.

Three minutes. Blue-bearded Carrie got claustrophobic and tried to get back out. There was a scuffle. Eli held one arm across the door and with the other fist he banged on the opposite wall and screamed at the top of his lungs: *Dad! Dad! Call it up!*

A voice came down the shaft. 'Murgh!' *5.4.3.2.1...* The elevator started like a tired donkey, with a long bray and a scrape.

It let them out straight into the loft – into Ethan's half of 5W, with its barred windows one foot from a grimy wall opposite. You always got the smell before you could see it: the processing chemicals he used to print the originals of the invites he designed. He was a typesetter. His rooms consisted solely of giant metal machines. And a sofa bed. Which they never saw him in. He was always at one linty swivel chair or the other, smoking while typing, or smoking while hovering over a slit robot mouth that dropped the long wet tongues of his stinky 'proofs'. He'd stick the ones he liked to the dust-layered stucco walls. As weeks passed, the paper oxidized and curled and turned amber and glossy, like fly paper. These hundreds of tongues made the walls look like they were shredding.

But tonight the place had been transformed: there was no other word for it. The smell was not gone, but it was certainly diminished, so much so that the children didn't need to rub their eyes. When they looked around from the elevator doorway, they were not aware, at first, of why they froze there. Redecoration wasn't in the lexicon of their experience.

Ethan Martian, the man himself – auburn Jewfro, tight jeans, skinny yellow tie – was in front of the hot-dog cart of a big blue typesetting machine (next to the fridge, across from the Xerox machine and the lightbox), tapping his foot in its bright new yellow-and-black Creeper. Smiling. The machines were turned off for the first time ever: they left a stunned silence. Gil was in the bathroom. The shower tinkled pleasantly, like a wee waterfall. As the shock diminished, the children regained their focus and saw all the 'feminine' touches that had made the difference: roses in an old olive oil bottle, the Palmolive without the coating of slime. Ethan's 'fave' shreds on the wall appeared to have been ironed, or at least brushed flat. There was a new wooden dish-drainer next to the sink, and a new yellow sofa bed with … sheets on it! The large poster that read I COULDA BEEN DUCHAMPION OF THE WORLD, usually the room's centerpiece, was shoved behind the machines. WORLD was all you could see. Carrie noticed that almost *any* detail you set your eye to was at least slightly altered. The light bulbs were peach-colored.

'The San Remo!'

Only a whole building of an Italian restaurant they had been begging Ethan to take them to for five years. It had Ionic or Doric or Corinthian columns (who cares!) made of stucco! Its sign was just a flag! It was on 9th Avenue; very whorey. The kids enjoyed walking past the hookers, watching them lean into drivers' side windows. They skipped to dinner, literally. All four of them. Gil and Carrie discussing jewelry and Ethan and Eli arguing about whether Stephen King sucked or not. Gil offered Carrie a pair of 'Art Deco' earrings from her delicate, cold ears. Carrie accepted. The streets got less and more seedy; they were passing Penn Station where a sign made out of lightbulbs announced a BOXING MATCH, YESTERDAY. Gil was clearly someone who knew how to make things clean, who bestowed earrings, and who had a hairstyle that wasn't ironic. Carrie made sure not to say too much. She didn't want to ruin what was obviously Gil's great impression of her. She wanted Gil to see and appreciate the Red Devil costume.

Gil kept interrupting Ethan who was in the middle of sentences like, 'But the thing is, man, King hates women. His agenda is normalcy not horror.' 'She is so preetty. Her mother must be beautiful. And also with zee blue cheen?' Gil was as lovely as she was forgetful. She repeated and repeated herself. 'How preetty her mother must be!'

'What am I meant to say to that?' said Ethan, beaming.

Next, Gil talked about how they were going to take Ethan's van and drive out to Califor-NI-AY next summer. Eli instantly managed to negotiate that the kids would get three dollars a day and eat *all* their meals in coffee shops. He had lists of the places he wanted to visit. Graceland, Great Adventure, Disneyland, The Texas Panhandle, LA Tar Pits, Mount Rushmore, Niagara Falls…

Inside, after being ushered into the empty restaurant by a snotty waiter in a red three-piece suit, bad acne and a handlebar moustache, Ethan ordered decisively. 'A banana daiquiri, heavy on the Capt'n Morgan's, and three Cokes.' When the guy was out of earshot, Ethan stage-whispered a quote from P.G. Wodehouse: 'Pimples OR a red bow tie, not *both*.'

Eli's father was smiling and clean and in a suit. Plans were being made for the summer vacation. Nothing like this had ever happened. Plus they were going to try to make the last show of *The Shining* at the Criterion Center in Times Square. Gil said she thought it sounded 'interesting'. Eli didn't know what face to make. He smiled constantly. His mouth hurt.

They read the torso-length twelve-page menus in reverential silence. Looming above, the walls rose to their three-storey height, a trap of gory, red, textured velvet paper, a red-on-red *fleur-de-lis* pattern. Here they finally were. They had arrived, here: just up from Madison Square Garden, just down from that Coliseum of snail-colored brick, the Greyhound Bus Terminal, encircled with sequined hookers. The San Remo felt like a restaurant in Capital City on a soap opera, with its chandeliers and its red checked table clothes. Eli was accompanied by a dick-length, bald, legless plastic man he'd picked up at Paper House the Party Store, in the joke section. When you squeezed him, his black eyes and red nose and lips popped out of his face. When you let go they were sucked up again.

Thirty-five minutes later, oxidizing on the table were four empty banana daiquiri glasses, six Mae West shaped drained Cokes, three large stuffed mushrooms and two T-bone steaks. During the meal there had been three renditions of two songs: '11:59' by Blondie and 'Mongoloid' by Devo, and two 'Dead Baby' jokes. The list of places they would visit on their trip cross country had swollen: Cape Canaveral, Death Valley, Albuquerque New Mexico, the hotel where *The Shining* was shot, which they thought was somewhere in Colorado. Carrie's minor objection – her fear of homesickness – had been shot down by Gil, who promised to take her shopping in Beverly Hills. This was bigger than Halloween, as Look-Forward-Tos went. This was unprecedented. What kind of kids go away on a trip in a van and live on coffee shop food? Not these two. This would *transform* them. Carrie rearranged the piles of things she kept in her head, all those dusty little sentimental objects – some real and on her dresser at home, and some ideas about herself, her mind, her life. Who *was* she, now that she was going to CA?

When Ethan went to the *twallette*, Gil followed. The kids watched the grown-ups shakily navigate the wrought iron spiral staircase that ran up the center of the room. Then Eli said, pointing at the mushrooms that had tasted like hamster litter, 'Should have got the veal-in-a-box'.

Night had fallen on 9th Avenue. The dining room glowed orange and scarlet. They watched a rare double decker bus pass outside – TORTURE IS BARBARIC was painted on the side in all caps – then Eli said dreamily, 'Arnie said we'd hitch a ride on one of those. He had this idea about jumping on the back, somewhere up in the Bronx, hiding for a while until it was crowded, then getting up on top. You know what they're doing there? In the bathroom? Don't you?' The wee man's eyes had been forced out for some time.

Over in the corner, the waiter was smoking a cigar and reading *Corriere Della Sera*. The ristorante was still empty. Two grubby children at a table alone in a bad restaurant/ money laundering operation, with big chandeliers, 1982. Carrie wanted to adhere one of the mushrooms at a jaunty angle to the wee man's head, but didn't know whether Eli would take kindly to it.

'No, eh? They're snorting coke. And *maybe* fucking. In the twallette. God you're out of it.' He threw the little man and it bounced off her head; they both giggled. 'Don't you hear anything? Don't you see anything? They didn't eat.' Eli lifted both steaks up on forks and slapped them together, while double-checking that the waiter wasn't watching.

'They said … she said she didn't feel well.' Carrie was under the table picking up the little man. When she came up, she put one of the mushrooms on his head and handed it back to Eli.

The little man said 'Grazie Signorina. Merci Mademoiselle. Gracias Chica!' They both started to laugh when the mushroom slid slowly off his head. By the time the coked-out-of-their minds post-coital adults returned nine minutes later the kids were in hysterics, pushing each other and laughing, their eyes tearing. They headed out to see *The Shining*.

On the way up to the Criterion Center at Times Square, Carrie asked Ethan about her boarding school application essay. She said, 'You were a professor. What do good schools like?'

'Make sure you get Viv to type it. You can't spell for shit.'

'I will. But I'm working on the *subject*. I was going to do something about how I always put the clean laundry back in the hamper, because it gets dirty right away at Mom's. And then Mom gets mad at me. But it seems to just get dirty right away. The second it's in the house, it's dirty.'

Ethan gave her a concerned and puzzled look. There was a long pause.

'That's a horrible idea.' He snorted in his good natured way and put his arm around Gil, who looked uncomfortable.

'Well I want to write something true. Helena said I should write about your divorce. She says these places love all that. But you're still married, right?'

'Zat does not matter.' Gil was positively sulking. Carrie realized with horror that she had managed to single-handedly ruin the evening. But *how*? There was so much to learn!

Ethan was oblivious to Gil's mood-shift. Eli was skipping uptown. It was only a matter of time. But Carrie couldn't just stop the conversation.

'Well just tell me what to write about.'

'Something sad, but not weird. For example: it's irrelevant that we're still married, and it overcomplicates it: so if you were writing about being traumatized by your parents' divorce – which would be a lie but who cares – it would just confuse the reader to mention the fact that we were married. Get it?'

'No.'

'Write about when Nora died.'

'Nora's not dead! Vera died! Nora is only two!'

'Course. Write about that.'

'I did have a scary dream about a boy. A dead boy. It was at your parents' house in Rhinebeck.'

'It's not in Rhinebeck, fuckface! It's like three fucking miles

130

from Rhinebeck.' Eli called from ahead.

Gil shrugged Ethan off.

He followed her over to a plate glass window in front of a bright empty office building lobby with giant ferns in the corners. The walls were a glossy cockroach brown. They leaned against the glass, half-hugging, half-arguing. It didn't look good.

The kids waited on the corner of 39th and 6th. Eli was tapping on one of those iron, light-changing boxes. Carrie was circling her toe one way, and then another, imagining semicircles. Eli whispered, 'What's fucking taking so long.'

Ethan came over and said, 'Tonight's not gonna happen. We can't make the show.'

Eli screamed and started crying. 'FUCK YOU!' He took off, running uptown. Ethan turned the corner and headed west, in a move that made it seem he knew the corners his son would turn, and how to cut him off. Carrie stood where she was, watching one and then the other. They both ran awkwardly, like large flightless birds; knees knocking, coats flying like obsolete wings. When she could barely see them anymore, she went over to Gil, who was standing smoking a Gauloise in the light of empty lobby of the office building.

'Do you fink it's ze breakup? Your parents?'

'No, that was lightyears ago. It's *The Shining*.'

Gil and Carrie walked back to the loft and came in to find Eli and Ethan already there, having met up and cabbed it. Eli was on the bed. The line up was starting on NBC: *Love Boat, Fantasy Island, 11 o'clock News, Saturday Night Live, Benny Hill*. Ethan had turned on the hot dog machine and sat smoking and typing. Everything back to normal. An inch of dust had fallen in two hours. Through a slightly opened door came the roar of Ethan's roommate Daisy's band practice. Eli had to wait to say hi until it was over: no males were allowed. Gil and Carrie went in to watch.

The band was practicing in the dark. You could see the big silver heads of the mikes and some pale shoulders slipping out from sweatshirts with the necks cut off, but that was about it. The amps were turned up so loud they gave you a stomachache. Carrie went as far away as she could, to her usual perch by Daisy's window; Daisy had the view-half of 5W. The Empire State building was lit up in Halloween colors. Across 28th there was a restaurant called A Deli Named Desire which was always shut, because it was a weekday lunch joint for garment workers. The sign was lovely, a deep blue awning with cursive words. The D was much larger than any of the other letters. Daisy said it was a shame Carrie was never around when it was open, because they had very good soup. It hurt to look at the awning for too long, though, because you had to lean way out and look straight down. When Viv used to drops the kids off, Carrie would lean out like that, and watch her walk away, back to the subway stop. She would wait until Viv got to the corner, and Viv would wave her arms and motion for Carrie to go in because she didn't like her leaning that way. Daisy was about Arnie's age. Carrie picked a book up off the floor under the windowsill, one that always seemed to be lying around: *The Basement*, Kate Millet.

Eli had read it and told Carrie all about it. A boy and his mother kept a little girl locked in their basement and carved things on her body, and starved her and raped her and finally killed her. Daisy told Carrie, 'Nothing will ever happen to you with General Daze around.' And it was true – Eli gave Carrie *zero* shit when General Daze was around. General Daze was Daisy's alter-ego: an old man with a thick Chicago accent who told stories about when beers were a nickel and about the time his Chihuahua got run over by a Raleigh three-speed bicycle. Carrie really wanted to go home, too. She usually wanted to go back to Viv's as soon as they got to her dad's. Once the movie was over, or the pizza, or the installation, or the gig.

She missed her mom the way a baby would. She would cry and cry and cry, and pine and pine. Eventually Ethan would be high enough to take offence, but by then it was time to go home anyway. Carrie figured the San Remo had been a reprieve; her crying would fly by. She'd be uptown in no time. Still she started to cry, by the window, holding the book and rereading the jacket. Daisy's band seemed to be getting *worse* the more they practiced. Their shittiest song was probably a rendition of 'The Girl from Ipanema', but 'Monkey Ghost' was pretty bad too.

When the Empire State shut off Carrie knew it was midnight. She went into the bathroom and sat on the closed toilet under the umbrella that was attached to the open ceiling to catch a leak from a pipe. She held the yellow phone in her lap, and tried calling her mother, over and over again. It was busy. Finally, after fifteen minutes or so, she called the operator: 'Can you tell me if there is trouble on the line?' 'Yes, there are no voices. Would you like to report a fault?' said the nice-sounding black lady operator. 'No thanks.' Carrie sat on the toilet seat for a while, weeping, imagining horrible things á la *The Basement* happening to Viv. Then pulled herself together and went back to say hi to Daisy.

Practice was over. The lights were back on, and Daisy was high on a new drug. Sweat ran down her pretty face. She was wearing aqua tights, an aqua beret and lots and lots of make-up.

'Carrie, it's like, *you*. It turns you into a kid again! I love it. It's called Adam!'

'Adam?' Carrie said, 'Why not Larry? Or Joel?'

Gil peeled off the wall, looking at the lesbian band like they had something sticky on them, and explained that Ethan was in a funk, and that they needed to go out to Marilyn's post-opening party because they had some coke they had to deliver to her, and if they didn't she'd probably start detoxing on the spot if she hadn't already. Carrie had noticed the sausage-shaped coke earlier on the lightboard. Ethan explained: someone had swallowed a rubber glove full of cocaine, got on a plane, and shat it out at La Guardia! It was funny watching Gil try to relate to Daisy. She was afraid of Daisy. She stood too far from her. Could Daisy watch the kids, so she and Ethan could get to the party?

General Daze thought it would be fun to walk the kids uptown to Viv's. She said it'd put hair on their chests, and she hadn't seen Viv in a while. Eli had to be torn away: he tried insisting that he could stay on his own – he was missing the Blues Brothers sketch on *Saturday Night Live* he'd waited the whole line-up for! In compensation, he demanded endless General Daze adventures. One time on the South Side, a lady tried to sell the General a bum pinball machine – a *Dukes of Hazzard* one, no less. It was bust beyond repair and General Daze had to get her money back. But *how*…

Then Daisy remembered something. 'You guys know Marilyn, the photographer? Where Gil and Eth just went?' Daisy pulled the cigarette out of her mouth as if it were stuck. (She also smoked True Blue 100s, just like Miss Rosa.) She had her face turned up to the sky, where a laser spotlight somewhere was pointed up. It panned from one side of Manhattan to the other, and Daisy/Daze followed it with her red eyes.

'The cokehead?'

'Anyway she asked me to ask you, Carrie, if you wanted to pose for this project she's doing called *The Sex Lives of …*'

'Does it pay?'

'Maybe twenty bucks. But she's very famous, her stuff's in MOMA. I mean if you *did* want to model, like Brooke Shields.'

'The Sex Lives of *what*?' asked Eli.

'Children. *The Sex Lives of Children.*'

'What the fuck kinda of fucked up shit is that, Daze?'

'What are you the fucking Moral Majority all of a sudden, Eli? Anyway, Carrie, it's just posing. I dunno. The construction of sexuality – something about that. You wouldn't have to have sex or anything! Gawd. She described something with you, like, putting on lipstick and then there would be a little boy standing behind you watching…'

'I'd do that shit.' said Eli.

'No, she didn't say *you*. Has she even met you?'

'Only a million times when we had to go bang on her door to wake her up. Shit.'

When they got home around 2am, Viv was passed out in Eli's loft bed, of all places. The phone was off the hook in a potholder where the old dishwasher used to be. The kids pulled out the sofa bed in the living room, and Eli slept on it. Carrie went to her own bed and fell asleep in her clothes. She woke up at 5am, disoriented. Phil Silver's light was on over the courtyard, and he was at his desk, shirtless, typing away. She could not remember why she was not in Rhinebeck, and then why she was not at her dad's. She walked the three paces to Eli's room and climbed up the ladder to his loft bed. Her mother and Daisy, both naked. Daisy's eyes were open. 'Come here' – she held her finger towards Carrie – 'Smell this. Know this smell.'

'Yeah.' Carrie climbed down the ladder and went back to bed.

The next morning she asked her mom if she was a lesbian. Viv was at her post, rolling a joint at the kitchen window.

'No.'

'Then why were you in bed with Daisy naked?' Carrie had to whisper because Daisy was in Eli's room playing Atari with him.

'She wanted to but I said no. I was so drunk. Grandpa Martian is giving us less money because he thinks Arnie lives here. Doesn't that just beat all.'

It was eleven am. Carrie had slept through the Saturday morning cartoon line-up, including the climax, *The Smurfs*. Her mother was so hungover she *still* had a southern accent, or had at least acquired a bizarre new vocabulary. *Beat all?* Alittlebitta Kentucky, right here on the Upper West

Side. Carrie headed out to Tony's for an Orangina. It was so bright out. Daisy wanted a Heineken and Viv a Sunkist (she had never had one, she giggled, cutely). Eli wanted *Fangoria*. Carrie said maybe she'd wear Tony down with her persistence.

At Tony's, Miss Rosa was lurking in the corner by the dog food and the porno mags. She had on heart-shaped sunglasses with black lenses. She held a long, skinny, white blind person's cane.

'Ah, you have your briefcase today. I have some good things for it. Come up, dear?'

Carrie did. And got the best part of the story to herself! Who says the worthy aren't honored? Who says they don't achieve fame in the eyes of 'gods and men'? Who says?

15. Spontaneous Lactation

THIS IS THE best part of the story. They used to make daisy chains. They were like a couple in love. Phoebe and Lavender forever. They went over the hill, past the shack, and down to the shore of the pond that Cyrus refused to take the muck out of; he said it enriched it. They came out looking like the creature from the Black Lagoon, but they all bathed in it. Lavender had skin ... his skin was the color of toffee, his eyes were like new willow leaves. The longest black eyelashes, like cricket's legs. His palms were small, and his fingers long too – and before Phoebe had finished explaining how to make the daisy chain, he could do it faster than she could. She had always said crafts bored her, that the real reason they didn't end up at Byrdcliffe was simple: they weren't artistic. *Art* bored them. But now ... Phoebe just wanted to be wherever Lavender was. In two weeks they made an endless daisy chain, it looped all over the lawn. Lavender was only five, but he spoke as well as Arnie. Lucy thought it was from reading him the King James Bible all the time. She thought ... it might just drop off, if she was lucky. Phoebe and Lavender forever. They stripped the grass around the pond and walked beside the brook, hand in hand. Lavender picked and talked. His voice like a bubble. He called her *Miss Phoebe*. His mother had not taken him off the tit. She thought it should be the child's choice. Hilda, Cy and Phoebe thought this was mad, but here was a black woman who thought a white God sat in heaven and would decide her eternal fate. For Lucy the world was a big mad puzzle, everything had to be made to fit, could be made to fit, what the Bible taught. If something came up, anything, she could

137

tell you in which book it was all explained, and what you were meant to do.

Hilda told Phoebe that when Lavender was born Cyrus had come running down the hill screaming, 'It's a ... both! He... She... has *both*!'

She. He. Just words. Lavender Johnson, *that's* more than words. Lucy usually stayed as far from Pondweed as possible, but for the first year of Lavender's life, she came to dinner down at Hilda's. She even drank the black fruit booze Cy made. She cried to Hilda and Cyrus, told them it was *their* fault: the fault of their ungodly union. They were all being punished with Lavender's *both*. Hilda said everyone knew Lucy could have married a white man – she was *that* hi-yellow – but for some bizarre reason she chose Cyrus. He polished up well, and poor Lucy had met him the *only* time he went to church. He liked pretty girls, and that was the end of that. He asked, and she said Yes. And Cyrus was lovable. Not as lovable as his son, though. Lavender spoke at six months: Milk, Horse, Moon.

One day, when Lavender and Phoebe were down by the pond, working on their chain, he tried to suckle. He did. And ... milk came out! Bright orange milk. The sky was purple. It was dusk. A hot-air balloon appeared above them, huge. Slow and huge. The evergreens closed up so high above them. Lavender and Phoebe and the balloon. He'd got under her shirt (one of Cy's – Phoebe was in men's clothes, as was often the case). Bright orange milk. Suddenly. She loved the size of him.

For some reason Phoebe said to Carrie, 'You have never had a moment's peace.'

Around that same time Hilda and Cy were up at Byrdcliffe one evening, taking a weaving lesson with a lesbian couple Hilda was trying to seduce. Lavender and Phoebe were late in town, on an errand. They ran into Lucretia at the haberdasher's. She nearly vomited when she saw him. She spat at him. That was the last time Phoebe saw her mother. Some people don't want to know the truth; they cling to their fictions for dear life, they kill for them … and it's not as though we can ever know. It's too intricate here to know *anything*. We are God's daisy chain. There is no natural. There are no abominations.

Phoebe peed on her chair. She hoped it would be short but it came and came and soaked it, and dripped onto the floor.

'Carrie?'

'Um hmmm?'

'Do you like poetry?'

'Yeah it's OK.'

'Listen to this. I wish I could have taught it to Lavender. He loved 'Ozymandias'.'

'Is it long?'

'No. It's over in a flash. Ah hem. "During Wind and Rain". Thomas Hardy.' She pulled the quilt over her head and sang the poem.

They sing their dearest songs –
He, she, all of them – yea,
Treble and tenor and bass.
And one to play;
With the candles mooning each face…
Ah, no; the years O!
How the sick leaves reel down in throngs!

They clear the creeping moss –
Elders and juniors – aye,
Making the pathways neat
And the garden gay;
And they build a shady seat…
Ah, no; the years, the years;
See, the white storm-birds wing across!

They are blithely breakfasting all –
Men and maidens – yea,
Under the summer tree,
With a glimpse of the bay,
While pet fowl come to the knee…
Ah, no; the years O!
And the rotten rose is ripped from the wall.

They change to a high new house,
He, she, all of them – aye,
Clocks and carpets and chairs
On the lawn all day,
And brightest things that are theirs…
Ah, no; the years, the years;
Down their carved names the raindrop plows.

Carrie stared at the lump under the quilt. 'He *dies*?'

He died. It was a few days after the spitting incident. Phoebe went away for the weekend, to teach spirit communion at Byrdcliffe. They were paying. Five dollars. It was her first attempt at paid employment since the unpleasantness at the Apthorp. She conducted a séance, and arranged for Cyrus to sneak up and rattle the drawing room windows. She'd brought some prints of girls sitting on moons and stars, and photos of ancient artifacts; fat faceless female torsos – and left them under their pillows, for these girls up from the city, who came to learn about mystery. They paid her with a bill with a picture of President Harrison on it. She still has it. She never spent it. It seemed like bad luck.

'It's there, under the conch shell on the mantle. Take it. Put it in your case.'

When she got home to Pondweed, they said he was gone.

He had fallen. And hit his head. The three of them stood in a line, in front of the well. They were all in their Sunday best. They were all wearing neck-ties; women wore them in those days. They had just buried him, they said, next to the well. Phoebe didn't believe them. She said so. She went inside. It was a warm night, Indian Summer. She took the *Farmers Almanac* and a lamp, she wasn't sure why – and then she left out the back. She heard them follow her, come out to the end of the road, like three ghosts, but she didn't turn around. She planned it then and there. Never return. Blackmail Cotton because he was gay. (That part she felt a little guilty about, but she got over it.)

Phoebe heard his voice as she walked away. He was saying, 'Don't be too good Miss Phoebe.' Whatever that meant. He never spoke to her again.

Carrie stood up. She put her hand on Phoebe's shoulder under the blanket, gently. When she felt the slight pressure, Phoebe flew into a full-body spasm so violent she crashed to the floor, knocking Carrie down on the way. Phoebe grabbed hold of Carrie by her blue snot, and they were twisted together in a ball. They lay surprised and still for a second on the smelly rug.

'Just help me up. Just put me back.'

Carrie did, holding the little old lady by the elbow, the way she had seen people do on television. Being so close to her, Carrie could not believe the stink of pee or how light Phoebe was. Carrie lay her down and stared at her. Her shades were pulled down and crooked on her nose. Carrie pulled the cover back over Phoebe's head.

'Is my rose light on?'

'No, it's bust. Are you OK? Are you going to be OK?' Carrie was so shaken, she held her imaginary Red Devil costume in front of her eyes, like a talisman. She saw a girl who looked like her, a little, but better. Thicker hair, honey-coloured instead of nothing-coloured. Shiny red unitard, sparkly devil's tail and horns. Not quite so skinny. A heart drawn perfectly on her cheek. She was winking, and wearing lipstick.

Phoebe didn't answer. She was asleep, breathing deeply. Carrie went quickly downstairs and out onto the 72nd Street.

She passed Tony's as Arnie was coming out. He had a black eye; he said it was all a mix up, and wouldn't say any more. They stood in front of a parking meter while Arnie unwrapped, tapped, then lit a Merit.

'What's wrong with you anyway? Why do you carry that fucking case everywhere? It's weird.' He looked at Carrie more attentively than usual. 'What's wrong?'

'Nothing.'

'Why are you crying?' He pulled his RayBans down on his nose.

'I'm not.'

Carrie told him about Phoebe falling, and he said he would check in on her. He was on his way to stop by Viv's. Just borrowing a joint.

Arnie turned and went east towards Miss Rosa's and Carrie headed west, then stopped abruptly. 'Arnie!' She ran back. 'She said that little boy died. *That they murdered him.* At my grandparents' country house. He's buried there. Under the well. No – it's true: they have the same house. And she pissed, she pissed all over the chair!'

Arnie hovered over Phoebe. He shook her awake. 'You gotta go to the doc's. What have you been telling Carrie? She's totally freaked out.'

'I told her the truth. Is that a fucking crime? You got hit, eh, Arnie? I can tell. You deserved it. *No one is here, Hilda. You can tell me why you did this to Lavender.*'

Arnie picked up the avocado-colored princess phone and dialed a guy he knew from Faggot Dock, a doctor. He lived on the 18th floor of the MacDonald's building. Arnie had gone across the street once or twice for a blow job while Viv slept.

Five minutes later the doctor came in with bloodshot eyes and his shirttails out. He reached up inside Phoebe. He pressed on her belly from the outside and Phoebe farted.

Arnie didn't know what to do with himself, so he went down for Phoebe's favourite, the Buddha's Delight lunch special from La Estrella. When he got back he stood outside the open door eating her fortune cookie, which read: *Society prepares the crime, the criminal commits it.* He listened to the doc saying, 'Miss Curtis – I'll just do the Medicare paperwork. We'll get a nurse here by 3 o'clock. I know a great Jamaican lady, who'll come before it's processed. She'll stay with you, if that is what you want.'

But Phoebe said, 'I don't want her. I've known far too many people already.'

16. A Termination

ARNIE LAY ON top of Lucy and said, 'You know, honey-bunch. I have fucked far too many people in my short life.'

Lucy weakly tried to pry herself up. 'Get off. I know I kept that witch hat.'

'Nah.'

She wanted to look in her closet and see if she had saved the hat from last year. She would wear it for Halloween, with spandex pants: a disco witch. She and Arnie were getting ready to go out for breakfast. Arnie was going to have a Spanish omelet. Lucy was going to have pancakes with vanilla ice cream. They'd been getting ready to go to breakfast for four hours.

Fifteen blocks uptown but also on the East side, Viv lay on her back, knees up, in an operating theatre at the Ladies First clinic. She stared at a poster on the ceiling of James Dean as her insides were quickly cleared of the embryo that would have been a boy. What if any thought, any addition we make to the fact of the present, is *always* a form of fiction? It can make you sick to your stomach if you think about what would have to be removed, if you decided that there was no trustworthy apparatus with which to name or order life. Words are the only things with meanings.

Murray had made the monthly deposit: two hundred dollars less. While she paid the 100 bucks for the abortion, Viv thought of ways to mention to Murray that Arnie had *already* moved out. She could send Eli round and get *him* to accidentally let it slip. It was too funny. Viv would not have anything like enough, and could not live on what Ethan gave her. The fact that he used most of his typesetting earnings to fund his coke habit … She could hardly mention that to his parents. As she was leaving the clinic she was weeping about her lack of money, and was glad it looked like she was weeping because of the kid.

At the crosstown bus stop it was starting to pour. It all seemed too bleak. She only had roaches to disembowel and re-roll at home. She decided she would stop off at her pot dealer's interior design shop.

When she got home, she stood at the kitchen window and ceremoniously unsealed the Ziploc bag she'd bought on credit. She left her hood up and her wet sneakers on. The aroma of the moist half-ounce made her feel very happy and calm. They had four hundred to live on until December 1st. Rent was 380, due November 1st. But she had just received her first Visa card, with a thousand dollar limit. It would be OK.

Viv began rolling her joint, warming up, looking absently at Carrie's blank application to The Hotchkiss School. She lit a match and held it to her J – which flared, setting the page in her other hand alight. She grabbed the application and tried to fan out the fire, which made it worse. The fire now grew happily, its element found. Her face pale as ash, she threw it in the metal sink. Rain was pounding on the window. It was raining so hard you couldn't see out the window. As Viv fumbled for the tap, the application form crumpled and twisted, a little brown hand balling itself into a fist.

'Aw Fuck.'

Carrie had been trying to piece together the Red Devil costume in her room. She came into the living room doorway in an old red leotard. (It was crackly, the way polyester gets when it's been through the drier too many times.) A moulded plastic tail with a fork at the end hung down between her legs, like a long crap. On her head was a pair of fine sequined horns. Daisy had given her them. She'd felt very guilty about the finger thing.

At the sight of Carrie, Viv could not not laugh. Now the

kitchen window was steaming up. Viv was boiling water in a saucepan for a cup of Weight Watchers instant soup she'd bought on sale.

'I don't have any red tights.'

'Wear your ballet ones?' Viv's eyes were watering. She sputtered a lungful of pot smoke.

'What's so fucking funny?' Carrie laughed too. 'Where's my application? That pot smells funny.'

'Oh honey … I just. I set it on fire.'

'It's not fucking funny! I'm supposed to mail it tomorrow! It said it has to be postmarked by midnight tomorrow! That's the deadline for financial aid!'

'Well I hadn't filled out the tax forms yet anyway. Neither has dad. He and I have to do it together. Because we file jointly.'

Carrie ran into her room and slammed the plywood door. It had lots of scrapes and holes in it from the locks she'd bought at the hardware store, and screwed in herself. Over the years Eli had removed them by various means. Her side of the door had also been spray-painted at one point. There was a large splotch in neon pink, and under it was written *Carrie's First Period By Eli*. Carrie slid down the back of the door.

Viv felt a rush of blood between her legs and a cramp in her stomach like a punch with brass knuckles. Pot's weird with physical sensations: it by no means makes the pain pleasant, but it does *expand* on everything, and adds a kind of kaleidoscopic filter. It does it with thoughts, too. Basically, it's distracting. Its aim is to constantly sidetrack, which is not necessarily a bad thing. Viv put her hand on her stomach. She made her way to the rejected loveseat and lay down with her feet on one arm and her neck on the other, and her hands over her eyes.

At the count of one hundred, Carrie ran out of her room. En route, she grabbed the Ovaltine-colored bathrobe that she and Eli shared. She raced down the back stairs, onto the pavement and around the corner in her bare feet. The street door was propped open. Maybe someone was moving things out? Carrie went up. Phoebe's apartment door was open too. Phoebe was in mid-sentence, in her chair, wearing the same turban and sunglasses she had had on when Carrie left Saturday morning. It was Wednesday, October 27th. Phoebe looked better: she was sort of glowing, iridescent, like a fish. It smelled like fish.

'…totally on my own. I'd always felt crowded, and I came to this apartment, and I had a small amount of money. I walked in Riverside Park before they built the Henry Hudson Parkway. I literally "watched the seasons pass" and the fashions change and the buildings get knocked over and the new ones put up again. I kept thinking I would get very lonely. I had no one to measure myself against, but that was easily solved by a trip to St Agnes Library, or a shop; a little human interaction goes a long way for me. I was normal enough. I read stories, I read poems, I went to the movies. Nothing realer. Those are funny things – the things that are supposed to be about people, but are really just *for* people. Then my money ran out, though I had been canned-soup-frugal …'

Carrie cleared her throat. 'Can I use your phone? I wanna call Helena to see if she has any ideas about how to improve my costume. You wanna see my Halloween costume?'

'Can't see! Gone blind!' Phoebe laughed, and peed. The ex-ballroom stank to high heaven. Everything smelled of cigarettes too in those days, so that's not even worth mentioning. OK? This whole book stinks of cigarettes.

'I always saw this window as sort of too *public*' – Phoebe reached behind her, and touched it, her fingers spread in as big a circle as she could make; they left little grease marks – 'I thought of myself as an imaginary public figure, in hiding … lord knows where that came from. Probably life at the movies. You start to think you're *in* a movie, always being watched. Plus I've always dressed theatrically.'

'Can I *tell* you how this looks and you can tell me if it sounds OK?'

'Go on.'

Carrie thought about it. 'Umm…' then spoke very slowly, as if she were writing down each word. '…*in the center of the pale green room with the big glass window, beyond the shiny red kitchen where cockroaches crawled unseen in the cabinets. stood the girl, four feet from the crystal ball. She was pale as a silverfish. She was thin as a blade of wheat. She wore a red leotard of her mother's that sagged at the ass and was pulled down further still by the plastic tail, which she had sewn, slightly askew, to her right buttock. Under the leotard she wore salmon pink ballet tights with the feet cut off. She had stolen her brother's tube socks, but they were in her drawer at home. On her head was a pair of stuffed red-sequined devil's horns from the Party Store.* Soooo? Do I look satanic or what?'

Phoebe was laughing. When she got her breath she said, 'Honey: you *are* satanic.'

17. Chapter Zero

VERY EARLY ON the day of the Halloween Parade, Arnie was heading east on Greenwich Street, feeling satanic. It was bright and freezing cold and he'd snorted a lot on the grave-yard shift under Gristedes on Bleeker. Downtown. Guys and gals with two-foot, sky-blue mohawks. When was it? Last night, before work? The night before? He'd been in the bath-room at the Mudd Clubb and it was so dark it was like being inside a car at night on a country road outside Princeton, where you would have stopped to roll a joint or fuck a girl. A man came into the dark men's room after him, handed him a card and walked out. His white Izod was bright pink in the blue lights. The card read 'AFTER HOURS'. Was it last night or the night before? Fuck! Time flies!

He and Lucy had left the club around 5am: he remem-bered the image on his Casio, the segmented 5 and 0s. On the 6 train back uptown to Lucy's apartment, she'd fallen asleep, her head on his shoulder. She had the sweetest breath in the world; it came through her parted lips in a tiny stream. Her place was always in order: carnations in vases; two stacks of bills, paid and unpaid; her panties care-fully clipped up to dry on a rack over the tub. She didn't seem to notice the anger and lust of the club, or of sex, even. She lived inside a pretty picture. At her place, he put her into bed, then watched her sleep. The sun rose behind him. From Lucy's bedroom window he could see the sky chang-ing color over Central Park. He turned from her sleeping face, and watched the sunrise go through the shades of a healing bruise.

Last week, when he'd tied Lucy's arms to the shower rail

with his shiny tie they were both laughing. The tie slid off right away.

Viv. Viv had taken less kindly to it. 'What the fuck you doing *that* for?' That was that.

If he got on the train right now and went up to Viv's for a nap, he'd have six hours till his next shift. And after that, the Parade. He needed to think. Yeah: it was only yesterday. It must have been yesterday he left Lucy asleep in her bed and got back on the 6 train and went downtown.

Today, on this bright Halloween morning, he's standing in front of Paper House the Party Store – the downtown branch. Ten minutes to nine. There's a bald scratch-headed mannequin in RayBans and a bat-cape – arms outstretched, turn-able wrists with suicide seams facing the ceiling, in the manner of a supplicant – in the center of the shop window. Around the dummy, in arcs the colors of the rainbow: post-cards, ribbons, novelty mugs, all suspended with string. The black backdrop and bright light of the clear morning give Arnie his reflection back. His beard is growing. His dirty dirty-blonde hair stands on end. Watching himself, he takes an expressive drag (a trick he learned from Viv) on his Merit, and then a postcard of a little girl catches his eye; it's falling from the precarious arrangement. It flutters and lands face up on the floor. A reproduction of the 1950s Coppertone Ad. A little puppy is pulling on a little blonde girl's towel, and her butt is white in the shape of a missing bathing suit. She looks back at him, dimpling, frustrated, from the card. She will live on the card forever. Just now, no, yesterday – it was confusing, because he had gone straight from the after hours club to the all-night shift that just ended – Arnie could tie up, gag and fuck a guy who *needed* it. Girls seemed to need something it cost nothing to give.

He pushes decisively at the door of Paper House. It won't open. A man behind the glass touches his wrist where a watch might have been under his sleeve. Arnie raises his hands in prayer, hunches his shoulders and makes puppy eyes.

'Ach, all right,' says the man to himself as he unlocks the door.

'How much is the bat-cape in the window, the one with the hood like a monk?'

'Thirty dollars.'

'Whoa. Can I try it?'

Arnie swings and flaps the cape. He runs through the aisles of crepe paper and fake dog shit and sequined masks. Swinging. Flapping. Twirling. He stops, breathless as a fat fifty-year old man, because he has been on coke for three days straight. He stands in front of a mirror then pulls the big hood down low.

'If you practice hard enough you'll fly.' The salesman is wearing a thick brown polyester three-piece suit. He lights a cigarette while Arnie pays, and then starts humming the tune to Fame. *'Fame – I'm gonna live forever. I'm gonna learn how to fly – high!'* As he turns the key to let Arnie out, the salesman shivers ostentatiously and says, 'It's a cold one.'

Viv's was the place to go. Two weeks ago the thought of it was stifling, but now the idea of doing the 'usual' – pacing around in front of the mirror, heating up an 'emergency' can of Broadcast corned beef hash, jerking off, showering with Dial, watching *People's Court* – felt like going home.

The 1 train was empty. As he walked towards Viv's, towards the river, 72nd Street was bright and windy. Gristedes' window was filled with masks and candy.

In the elevator he could hear the wind above him in the shaft, whipping around. Or was it from the roof? Suddenly he had a sense that he was not inside, ever. That the whole idea of there being places that were inside and places that were outside was some weird hoax. He pushed open the door on *both* the fucking kids.

'We're sick.' Carrie was sitting at the table in front of an auspicious looking pile of *New York Times*es. Eli was on the couch in the Ovaltine-colored robe, glowing lobster red, just out of the bath.

'Shrinkydinks. Wanna make one?' She points to the baking tray on a breadboard in the center of the table: little curled up bits of translucent plastic shaped *sort-of* like Snoopies and Garfields and Vampires. A few heads detached from bodies, an axe with blood dripping down it.

Arnie collapses onto a rocking chair. 'I'll pay you five bucks to heat me up a can of hash.' Eli pushes Carrie over as they race to the utensil drawer for the can opener.

'I have strep.' Carrie explains, falling back in her folding chair (another Martian hand-me-down), jamming a large disk of penicillin into a spoonful of Dannon coffee yogurt and swallowing it, while trying to see what face Arnie is making under his RayBans. 'But there is *no way* I'm not going to the Parade.'

Eli and Carrie have agreed that if her Snoopy-in-a-white-sheet Shrinkydink turns out indistinguishable from a booger ('It's *shrink*-ee-dinks, you gotta take that into account', was what Eli had argued; 'It's not gonna look like what you draw; the process will change it and you won't know, *no one* will know what the fuck it is!'), Eli will be allowed to put her in the pink sateen laundry bag, for three minutes, just to see what it's like.

Arnie has finished the hash, with loads of ketchup, and he stands, still in his sunglasses, in the bathroom doorway watching Carrie in her knee length *I Love NY* T-shirt as she steps into the empty bathtub, then into the bag. Eli quickly pulls the ropes, she laughs, and then he turns the cold tap on and shoves the pink blob under.

They have great water pressure being so close to the roof, and Carrie yells over the roar, 'No water! Just the bag! You fucker!' But she is laughing. Arnie grabs a toothbrush and a hairbrush and pokes the writhing bag saying, 'Yes, yes – a bit of moisture will help to make z'stew better. And now into the oven!' It's his Swedish-chief-from-the-Muppets impersonation. He lifts the mass high over his head and turns to the hall closet, flicking the switch with his hip.

The closet's like a landfill. A year ago Viv paid Arnie and Eli twenty bucks to clean it out. Then, in the four-foot-high pile of clothes they found: a civilization of silverfish feasting on children's books; maggots in a rotting cantaloupe; a baby blanket caked in dog shit; a stiff gold Dior dress (a gift from a real princess, who liked Viv's Tai Chi style); several mismatched high heeled shoes; thirty dollars in change; and the remains of a hamster, Otis, who had disappeared some years back. They left the closet immaculate, but one year on it has returned to its former glory. The pile may even be higher. Arnie wobbles on top of it as he places Carrie on the highest shelf, next to the old family albums, with photos of the kids when they lived in Santa Cruz for a year, when Ethan was still teaching. In those days Viv kept their big rented house clean and Ethan cooked spicy Mongolian food. They smoked 'very weak home-grown' and drank beer.

'Don't move or you'll roll off.'

Carrie feels the heat from the bare bulb in the ceiling. She doesn't really want to come down. She wants to just lie there curled up and warming up forever.

When Viv gets home after an appalling day at Macy's festive Halloween-themed Self Center, she finds the place empty. She puts on a cassette of *The Mikado* that she's been wanting to listen to, and lights a joint. The night is cold but she leaves the kitchen window wide: it was one of those fall NY nights with a smooth velvet blue, cold sky.

Here is Eli waving sparklers, their light mixing with the dove color of his breath, as he runs through the boom boxes and glitter of the crowd at the Parade. He already has tickets to the Halloween Midnight Showing at the Greenwich Twin. His eyes are shining. He's dressed as Jack Nicholson, a rubber axe bouncing off his head.

Here is Carrie in a doorway looking for someone, but she's become detached from the parade. She's clutching her *attaché* to her chest and blaming it for everything. It ruins the get-up. What is she – a Devil-slash-*lawyer*? After one minute 'lost', she decides to go home. She feels like she is in the lunchroom again, wondering what the roar is. What's all the fuss? The parade is moving but it's unclear where to. WHAT'S ALL THE FUSS? Luckily, Mayor Koch has declared all public transportation free tonight. She makes her way down the steps and onto the 1 train at Christopher Street. A man offers her a seat but she refuses, then he stares at her the whole ride, looking around to see if she is on her own. Some drunks sing the chorus from *Fame*. *'I Wanna Live Forever!'* As the straps sway from the ceiling and the train roars through Columbus Circle, the lights flash on and off. Someone pulls Carrie's tail off in the dark. When the lights come on at Lincoln Center, Carrie sees the man who offered her his seat sucking on its point. She gets off there, just as the doors are closing, so that if anyone has intended to follow her she'll lose them; she waits until the last second, then runs through the car and slips out through a crack.

She walks up to 71st, intending to go home (and she will eventually find the atmosphere there lovely and calm, with the cool night air, and the smell of sinsemilla, and Gilbert and Sullivan, and Viv quiet but lively) then carries on and turns down 72nd. In her leotard and tights and Nikes. She's taken the horns off. She climbs the cruddy stairs and pushes the door open. Phoebe's studio's empty. No sofa bed or table. No Moreno clown or Almanac, no conch. No shelves, no lamps. Long black cracks ran from the ceiling to the floor, like seams in stockings. No neon rose. No fish tank crystal ball.

Carrie sits down on the floor and opens her *attaché*. She takes out her Ben Harrison five, and a little photo of a woman in a corset, and another little photo of a black man in a top hat standing next to a white woman wearing a fake beard. She goes into her trance. But it's different, finally. Because when she is done being one with the air and the room and its noises, she recedes from the blankness and it's suddenly clear to her: that was just preparation. She sees a rainy funeral. She welcomes a casket, and a handful of mourners. They have paper plates on their heads, decorated with flowers made of Bamboo rolling papers. She wants to see their faces, but she can't. She can't make anything happen. After not very long she repacks her case, and goes home.

Epilogue

VIV AND CAROL were wearing the same dress. So why was it that Viv ended up with the bad luck that night, September 30th, 1966, her clothes robbed, raped by two men already notorious in the neighbourhood?

But Viv managed to outsmart them. She told Carrie this, about a week after Miss Rosa ceased to exist. Viv and Carrie were walking home after borrowing more money from Johnny Madrid.

'I don't tell you this to scare you, I just think you need to know that you aren't always safe. You can't really trust people. Well, there's not much to it. I accepted a cab ride with two guys. One small, the other giant, like Frankenstein. Like Dustin Hoffman and John Voight in *Midnight Cowboy*, that's a great movie, they play it sometimes on TV, or they'll probably show it at the Regency. It's a classic. Well – there's not much to it. I should not have taken the lift. They held a gun to the cabbie's head and told him they had to take us where they said. Then we went back to a penthouse on West End and they both had sex with me. I was OK, but I didn't want to. Then the little one fell asleep. There I was, in only my boots. He said if I tried to get away he would throw me off the roof. Can you imagine it, Carrie, naked, off the roof, with only high heeled go-go boots on? The big one, though, was dumb as a stone, and while the little guy slept I managed to convince him to get me some of the little one's clothes. High-waters and a tank top. I told the big one that while he was getting the clothes I had called the White House. Because I had my Driver's License on me, and Cox was also the last name of the Secretary of State – at the time. I said I was his daughter, and I'd told the White House if I wasn't home in ten minutes to start a search of all the penthouses on West End Avenue, because I didn't know exactly where I was. You know I used to act. It's actually a very useful skill – and when you need to use it, you can. The big guy was terrified. I can still see his face. So I went home. And *really* what bothers me most about that night is when I got home my cat, my Kookie, was dead. She'd fallen. The ledge was too old, and it just fell off. That's why we always keep the screens in. The guys? I tried to press charges, but these goons were very well connected – they always are. Let that be a lesson to you. Cats can't survive a fall. Do you want to get a frozen yogurt? I'm starving. Hey look there's old Lawrence Levy! Lawrence, come here – I'll get ya a slice.'